MW00943994

LIAM

MAMMOTH FOREST WOLVES - BOOK ONE

KIMBER WHITE

NOKAY PRESS LLC

For all the latest on my new releases and exclusive content, sign up for my newsletter. http://bit.ly/241WcfX

For the real Molly…

I'll be the eyes in the back of your head, my friend.

ONE

LIAM

I t's gotten easier to keep to the shadows. I seem to do it now without even thinking. It's not the light that bothers me. I thrive in it. We all do. On a day like this, with a full, bright sun softening the tar beneath my feet, it's so much harder to stay invisible. The shadows are the safest place to keep curious eyes from landing on me. And, they always do. I'd love to walk among you. Normal people, drawn by the blue skies and fresh air. It's the perfect day to walk downtown to shop, to eat, just to feel the sun on your face after such a bitter winter. Because, a cold Kentucky winter will come again soon enough, and there will be nothing but bleak shadows left.

I took a careful step into the sunlight. Downtown Shadow Springs consisted of four streetlights and ten city blocks. But, the population seemed to have doubled today. Two streets over, the local police began to block off three of those city blocks for the local street fair coming into town on the weekend. It's the kind of thing that draws people out of their office buildings just to come and watch. That made things perfect for me. Anything that could draw attention away from curious eyes as I strolled through town helped. The more I'm seen, the riskier it becomes for me to disappear.

I wouldn't have come out at all today except there really was no other choice. Jagger and the others warned me not to go, but there was no one else. Besides, what's one lone wolf strolling through town? As long as I didn't talk to anyone and I kept those curious eyes on me to a minimum, I could get away with one, maybe two hours topside before it got seriously dangerous.

Sure enough, most of the people downtown were headed east of me toward the town square. Booths and tents were being set up by the street vendors. It was the same fare every year, local artists, rib trucks, a mini-carnival. Still, it was unique enough to keep anyone from giving me a second look. I headed one more street over. The building I wanted was tucked between a barber shop and a payday loan center.

Shadow Springs Veterinary Clinic

The small C at the end of the sign was smashed out. The windows were dark. The office didn't open for another hour. I picked a spot across the street where I could watch the back entrance off the alley. This is where the employees would come in. Making myself as small as I could, I wedged myself in a corner between a giant blue dumpster and the brick wall on the south side of the Shadow Springs Laundromat. From there, no one could enter the back door of the vet clinic without me seeing them.

The walkie in my back pocket beeped. I reached quickly back and clicked off the volume. It would just be Jagger or Mac bitching at me to get back to the caves. I'd been gone over an hour already. Every minute I drew air up here put me at risk. Though I didn't sense any other shifters nearby, they could be getting better at masking, just like I was. It would only take one of them to sense me, and it would put all of us in grave danger. It was easier when the Chief Pack had orders just to kill us on sight. Now, we'd heard rumblings that their Alpha wanted us alive. That was one of the reasons this little recon mission was so important. Though none of us would give voice to it yet, we needed a doomsday option. I'd die before I let them take me. Any of us would.

I pressed my back further against the wall as a car drove up with a man behind the wheel. I sniffed the air, but he was human, not shifter. As soon as he parked, a woman got out of the passenger seat. She was tall, with straight hair dyed a shade of red that looked maroon in the sunlight. She wore it tied back and as she emerged, she twirled a lab coat and stabbed her arms through it.

As she shut the car door, her companion rolled down the passenger side window and leaned across the front seat.

"Don't shut your phone off today, Bess," he warned. I didn't like his tone. It was low, threatening, aggressive. But, more than that, Bess's back stiffened and she leaned in, gripping the window frame. She was scared. I could sense it rolling off of her, and a growl rumbled through me.

"Zeke, I've got two surgeries scheduled today. I can't keep my phone on me the whole time. But, I promise I'll call you before and after each one. Just relax, baby."

Zeke didn't relax. He got out of the car. Sweat started to trickle down the back of my neck, and my whole body started to vibrate. I curled my lips back and dug my fingers into the brick wall behind me.

Not now, wolf. Not now.

Zeke came around the car. Bess took two steps back. She had a nervous smile plastered on her face and when Zeke got close to her, she flinched. He hadn't even raised a hand yet, but still...she flinched.

I narrowed my eyes and tried to focus on my breathing. The hairs on top of my hand started to burn. Burn and grow coarser, pricking my skin.

Zeke put his hand on Bess. He gripped her upper arm and jerked her toward him. "Don't you tell me to relax. Who the fuck do you think you are?"

"Zeke, please. You're hurting my arm. I promise. I'll call you before and after both surgeries. The first one's at ten. It should take maybe two hours. The second is at two. That one's gonna last at least three hours. Baby, I'm not going anywhere else today."

Zeke gritted his teeth. He looked around, but he didn't see me. Of course he didn't. I blended into the shadows. I should close my eyes, I knew it. One glance in my direction and Zeke would be able to see two golden orbs as my wolf eyes flashed. I pounded the back of my head against the brick, anything to try and drive the wolf back. If he tried to hurt her…

Zeke jerked Bess toward him. She cried out from the pain and shrank, trying to make herself so small. Her eyes carried a haunted look, scared, defeated. Even from this distance, my wolf eyes showed me the tracks of her tears. Beneath that, though she tried to cover it with cheap makeup, Bess sported an old bruise just below her right cheekbone He'd backhanded her. I could make out the outlines of a jagged scar. A ring. It looked like something he got for playing football in High School or maybe college. Zeke wore it on his right middle finger.

"Is he going to be here today? Is that why you're trying to blow me off?"

"Zeke, please. I don't know what you're talking about."

He pressed his lips against her ear and whispered. Though they stood more than fifty feet away from me, with my keen wolf ears, I could hear everything he said with perfect clarity.

"Yes you fucking do. You better figure out a way to answer your phone if I call you today. I don't give a shit how. Have one of your useless technicians carry it in her pocket. You're a smart woman, *Doctor* Kennedy."

"Okay, okay. Fine. Yes. Zeke, yes. I'll figure something out. But you don't have anything to worry about. I swear. You know that. I've told you a thousand times. Now, I've got to go. I've got to prep for my first appointment."

He pushed Dr. Bess Kennedy, hard. She staggered and lost her balance. She got her hands out just in time and braced her fall against the opposite wall. Her palm scraped against the hard brick, breaking the skin. The scent of blood reached me, and my inner wolf went nuts.

Zeke was just a man. Just a vile shitheel of a man. He towered over Bess with his fists curled. Mixed in with Bess's blood, I could scent the adrenaline coursing through Zeke's veins. He laughed at her, called her clumsy, ordered her to get up and kiss him good-bye. He raised his fist and laughed even harder when she flinched.

"Get the fuck up," he said again. My inner wolf raged. God, if I shifted here in the street, I was done for. No way my scent wouldn't reach the outskirts of town. There were probably a dozen or more members of the Chief Pack just waiting to pick up my trail.

Zeke took a step closer. Bess cowered on the ground, her eyes batting wildly as Zeke hovered over her. His need to do violence poured off of him. He was throwing off something else as well. Not shifter, but he was altered somehow. He was under the influence of at least alcohol, but I suspected heroin or something else. Bess was in trouble...real danger. My wolf raged.

The backdoor to the vet clinic flew open. Another woman charged out of it wielding a baseball bat two-handed. She had brown hair, pulled back in a ponytail with bangs, cut straight across but hanging so low they almost hid her eyes. She raised the bat and took a swing at Zeke.

Zeke jumped out of the way at the last second and her swing landed with a hard crack against the wall.

God, she was little. She couldn't be more than five feet tall. The girl had fury in her brown eyes and she raised the bat a second time. Zeke was so stunned by her appearance and the first strike, he took two staggering steps backward.

"Molly!" Bess shouted from the ground. "Don't. Don't hurt him!"

"Are you kiddin' me?" Molly yelled back. She took another step toward Zeke then turned her head to the side and spit on the ground, aiming for his feet.

"Are you fucking crazy?" Zeke said, but he'd backed away from both women, raising his hands as if she were holding a gun.

Molly choked up on the bat and faked a swing. Zeke flinched and she advanced on him.

"Get in your car, you asshole," she said. "Now."

Zeke's bravado came back. He squared his shoulders, staying just outside the circle of danger from Molly's bat. "Settle down," he said. "Ain't nothing happening out here that's any of your business."

"Really?" Molly said, eyes flashing. The toned muscles of her biceps flexed as she snapped the bat back. She wore a black stretchy tank top with the words "Hot Mess" emblazoned across it in silver, glittery cursive. Her cutoff jean shorts were rolled up high enough that I could see the hint of her ass cheeks when I tilted my head. Her nostrils flared as she took bold steps toward Zeke.

"See," she said, her Kentucky drawl growing thicker as her anger rose. "I'd say what's happening out here is exactly my business, Zeke. Dr. Kennedy runs this place. I work at this place. You start wailing on her again then she can't see patients. Then everything goes to shit and I don't get paid."

She was incredible. Short, solid, filling out her tight jean shorts in all the ways I liked. A tiny line of sweat ran down between her ample breasts. The tank top she wore barely held them in. She had on cheap, canvas sneakers, ripped and frayed on the sides. Zeke towered over her by nearly a foot and probably had a hundred pounds on her, but little Molly didn't flinch. She white-knuckled that bat and kept right on coming.

"Get in your car," she said, spitting on the ground again. "Drive away, Zeke. Stay away."

Zeke straightened his back. He looked at Bess on the ground. Her jaw hung slack as she tried to figure out which of these two posed a bigger threat. The answer was neither of them. The biggest threat was me, lurking unseen just a few yards away.

"Remember what I said, Bess," Zeke said, moving toward her.

Molly swung that bat again, slamming it down hard on the hood of Zeke's Chevy pickup. It left a deep dent and she cocked her arm back ready to go again.

"Jesus Christ," Zeke yelled. "Crazy fucking bitch!"

He moved toward her, cocking one fist back even as Molly took a ready stance, raising the bat to her right shoulder one more time.

Zeke never got the chance to strike. My fingers closed around his wrist, wrenching it backward hard. He took an awkward step back, trying to relieve the pressure.

"The fuck?" he said.

The tiny hairs on the back of my hands bristled again. I stood with my back to Molly and Bess; only Zeke could see my eyes. His own widened in fear as he recognized the threat. Predatory. Danger-ous. Deadly. He knew exactly what I was even if he'd never admit it to himself. This was Shadow Springs, after all. Most of the humans around here would never say it out loud, but they knew.

Things weren't always what they seemed with people in this town. Zeke was a heartbeat away from finding out why.

"Hey, man," he said, still trying to twist his wrist out of my grip. "Back off."

"I think you need to back off," I said, shocked that I could still form words. My voice was low, barely more than a growl. Whether Zeke knew other shifters, I couldn't guess. But, he understood on some preternatural level that he was just inches from certain death if he didn't stand down.

"Let him go!" Bess shouted behind me. She'd found her feet again. I kept my eyes on Zeke. I knew what he saw in mine. To him, they'd glint gold, the pupils blacker and wider than any human's should be. I felt his pulse quicken beneath my grip as his fight or flight response kicked in.

"Get the fuck out of here," I said. "That's your best play, man."

Zeke nodded, his jaw dropping. I felt Molly's hot breath on the back of my neck. She stood close behind me, raising her bat. I wanted to think she still only meant Zeke harm. That was probably true, but she was smart to be wary of me.

"Ladies," I said, not sure I could keep the wolf in check for much longer. "Why don't you head inside? Zeke and I have everything under control here."

Molly had the presence of mind to recognize my tone. From the corner of my eye, I saw her help Bess to her feet. She rested the bat on her shoulder and put an arm around her friend.

"Yeah," Zeke said, trying to salvage his pride. "Get the fuck out of here. You're both fucking crazy."

"Thanks," Molly said. I didn't dare look at her full on. I couldn't let her see my eyes.

"Zeke, I'm sorry," Bess said. She tried to get around Molly, but for as short as she was, that girl was solid. She steered Bess through the back door, leaving Zeke and me alone.

I let go of Zeke's wrist. He drew it to his chest, rubbing it. "You're just as crazy as they are," he said.

"Maybe," I answered. "But I didn't like what I saw. You touch that woman...or any woman like that again, I'm going to know about it. We clear?"

I let the wolf out just enough so that Zeke understood. His eyes widened and his lips went white. Oh, yeah, he understood. In the back of my mind, I knew how dangerous a game I played. My vision started to go fuzzy at the edges. A pounding beat that began at the center of my forehead drew me back. I struggled to keep my mind blank. If I let myself go feral, the Chief Pack Alpha would know how to find me. One of his generals patrolled Shadow Springs proper. God, if only I knew who he was. For now, I could feel the Pack closing in. I'd stayed out way too long.

I couldn't breathe. The pull started low in my belly. God, it would be so easy to just succumb. My stomach flipped and sweat started to pour down my face. Zeke saw it. He knew something was wrong. I should have turned. I should have run. But, the command growing inside of me kept me rooted to the ground.

Stay. Don't move. Submit.

I couldn't heed it. I had to go. Now!

"You don't look so good, man," Zeke said. His eyes narrowed, and I sensed a new threat from him. I was powerless to ward against it. I was too busy fighting off the command that would lead me to disaster.

"Yeah, that's what I thought," Zeke said, growing bolder. He tore a hand through his hair and looked both ways across the alley. We were alone. No witnesses.

"Don't," I said. Zeke thought I was talking to him.

"Fucking junkie. Is that what you are? Big man. Sticking your nose in where it doesn't belong. Here, maybe this will help you remember to mind your own fucking business next time."

Two things happened at once. A flash of silver drew my eyes. Heat blossomed in my belly where Zeke stuck the knife in. The back door to the vet clinic opened and Molly stepped outside.

Zeke got spooked. My back was still to Molly, so I didn't think she could see. Zeke slipped his knife back into his jacket pocket and hot-footed it back to his pickup.

"Everything okay out here?" Molly asked. Blood poured from the wound in my belly. The wolf was coming out. There was no more time.

I stole one quick glance at her. I don't know what she saw. I couldn't risk sticking around a second longer.

"Hey!" Molly called after me. But to her, I was already a blur of motion, running back to the safety of the shadows.

TWO

MOLLY

I must have been losing my damn mind. My fists curled around Dr. Benny's baseball bat. He didn't work here anymore, but he'd left the bat behind, saying we "girls" could never be too careful.

"Hey!" I called venturing further into the alley. Dr. Kennedy's d-bag boyfriend squealed his tires as he backed up and drove down the street.

"Good riddance," I muttered under my breath as I leaned the bat against the wall and walked a few steps forward. Where in the hell was that guy? He'd come out of nowhere. It seemed impossible for a guy that big. He had to be six three, maybe taller. One giant hunk of muscle with ginger-brown hair and brooding eyes. He looked like he could have been a model on one of those politically incorrect cigarette ads they used to have in magazines. All leather jacketed smolder and testosterone.

I wanted to thank him. I had things well in hand with Zeke, but I knew damn well Dr. Bess was probably going to end up going home with that asshat later tonight anyway. I warned her last month if she came into the office with one more bruise on her that hadn't come from a bitey chihuahua, I was gonna use that very baseball bat.

All I found in the alley before me were empty shadows and hamburger wrappers from the fast food place down the street. "Pigs," I muttered. The damn dumpsters were two feet away. Actually, that wasn't fair to pigs. I picked the trash up, holding it as far away from me as I could before lobbing it over the side of the open dumpster.

That's when I saw the blood.

More accurately, I stepped in it. There was a lot of it, running in a small river until it filled a crack in the pavement. I jumped to the side, but I'd already gotten some on the side of my canvas Converse.

"Shit," I said, lifting my foot. No amount of bleach was going to get that out. "Are you back there?" I called out, knowing it wouldn't do any good. Cigarette Model Man was long gone.

Was this his blood? But Zeke hadn't touched him. The guy had moved so fast I didn't think Zeke even got close to him. My heart raced, wondering whether this guy had really gotten hurt.

"Molly?" The back door to the clinic cracked open and Bess stuck her head outside. Her skin was still pale and she cast a furtive glance down the street.

"He's gone, Bess," I said. "Hightailed it outta here. I don't know what that guy said to him, but it scared him good and plenty. Can't say as I'm too sad about that." I glanced back down at the trail of blood. It was the heaviest right where Zeke had been standing. Maybe I had it all wrong. Maybe *he* was the one bleeding. I know it wasn't charitable of me to think so, but I kind of hoped he was. He deserved it. Maybe he'd think twice about sniffing after Bess anymore.

"Come on inside, Molly," Bess said. She edged her torso into the space where she held the door open, but wouldn't step outside herself. I was glad. For some reason, I didn't want her to see the blood. She might worry about Zeke or try to call him.

"Yeah," I answered. I turned my body toward her but kept looking over my shoulder. I had the oddest sense that someone was watching me. A strange tingle shot straight down my spine.

"Yeah," I said again, quickening my step. "We're gonna have a hell of a time playing catch up if we get any later of a start."

Bess gave me a weak smile as I moved around her and went inside. It was just the two of us this morning. The rest of the techs wouldn't come in until a little later. I had to process at least three admissions this morning. Two dogs for X-ray sedation, a third coming in for a spay.

"Did we get the labs back on the Sphinx?" Bess asked. She walked next to me, chewing on her thumbnail.

"Just came through," I answered. "Everything looks good. As soon as they get her here, she'll be ready to go back. Jason and Lynette will be in by nine. I can do the rest of the prep work."

Bess nodded, still distracted by her thumbnail. "You should have had Lynette come in early. You don't have to handle all these admissions by yourself, Molly."

"Uh huh," I answered. Except Lynette had three kids she needed to get to daycare. Jason worked third shift down at the lumber mill before he came in. I was the only tech who was currently single, childless, and only working this job.

"Bess," I turned to her, blocking her path down the hallway.

Bess took in a great breath and leaned against the wall. "Don't," she said. "Not this morning, Molly."

"Right," I said, slapping my hand against my thigh. "Not this morning. Not any morning. What do you think would have happened if I hadn't been here, huh? Zeke was fixing to hurt you, Bess. Bad. Again. He's got a problem. He's not going to change. You're not going to fix him. Ever."

Bess was looking right at me, but she didn't seem to see me or hear me. All I got was a slow blink and a pasted on smile. It's all I ever got.

I let out a bitter laugh and shook my head. "I'm wasting my breath," I said.

"Molly." Bess reached for me, but I shrugged her off, turning to the front door. At the same time, Jason walked in from the back. God bless him for coming in early anyway. He was big, burly, standing over six feet and change and looked every inch the lumberjack he moonlighted as except for one thing. Jason Calhoun had a high-pitched soft voice. It worked wonders on the animals as well as half the humans.

"Molly!" Bess called after me again, but our three admissions were already lined up at the door. I shot a look back at Jason. He widened his eyes over Bess's head. He must have caught the tail end of our conversation. Dr. Bess's bad boyfriend was the office's open secret. He'd never change. She'd never leave him. And we all knew there was only one way it could end.

Later in the afternoon, as I checked Bess's post-op notes, Jason finally found me and asked for the details. I sat in the back office with my feet propped up on the desk and two stacks of files. Bess Kennedy liked to do everything the old fashioned way. She hated the tablets and preferred charting her notes with pen and paper. I was pretty much the only one capable of deciphering her hand-writing and digitizing everything.

"Thumper the cat is resting comfortably." Jason's sing-song voice echoed through the room. When I looked over my shoulder at him, I couldn't help but laugh. A diabetic since he was a little kid,

Jason was blind in his left eye. When he focused those brilliant blues at you, it gave him a look of permanent exasperation that was imminently endearing. Doubly so because Jason kind of *was* permanently exasperated.

He reached over me and grabbed the iodine out of the top shelf. "Yowza," I said. He had three red lines on each of his massive forearms. Thumper the cat must have gotten in a few swipes before he went down for the count.

"Here, let me," I said, dropping my feet to the floor. I grabbed the gauze and took the bottle from him. Jason plopped down in the chair next to me and held his arms out and gave me a pout. God, he looked like a giant toddler. I dabbed the gauze in the iodine and started to debride his cuts.

"So, what the hell did I miss this morning?" he asked, lowering his voice to a whisper. Bess was already gone for the day. It was just me and the other techs now. She claimed she was taking the bus home, but I knew it was a lie. Jason said he saw Zeke's pickup parked at the end of the street.

"Same shit, different day," I answered. "One of these days, that asshole is going to kill her. I don't even know what to do about it anymore."

Jason winced as I dabbed more gauze to his cuts. "She's in love with the fucker. Plain and simple. You know, her own family won't even talk to her anymore. I saw her sister-in-law a few weeks ago at the grocery store. They've thrown up their hands. Say they won't enable her bad life choices anymore."

I bit my lip past the mean things I wanted to say about Bess Kennedy's family. The Kennedys were big in this town. Money and power in local politics. "It makes me sick. She has everything. Went to college and grad school on her daddy's dime. He got her this gig right out of the gate when Benny retired. And she's willing to piss all over it and throw it all away over that loser.

Meanwhile…" I stopped myself. God. Watching Bess and Zeke Redmond seemed to bring out the worst in me.

"It's all right, you can say it," Jason said. "We're all thinking it. Meanwhile, the rest of us are barely scraping by. You're working two and three shifts covering for everybody else, including me. You live in a damn trailer park by the river and can barely afford that on the shit pay we get here. It's hard to watch, Molly."

I sat back in my chair and tossed the gauze into the wastebasket. I'd put sterile wraps around Jason's cuts. He held his arms out in an awkward Frankenstein-esque posture. When I gave him a nod, he rested them on the desk and gave me a sheepish grin.

"I just don't like seeing a nice person get shit on, that's all," I said. "I don't begrudge Bess Kennedy or anyone else any advantage they've ever gotten. We all have our own struggles. Nobody's life is any easier than anyone else's. It's just…"

"Yeah," Jason said. "Like I said, it's hard to watch. But did you really go after that douche-pickle with a baseball bat?"

I rolled my eyes. "Well, somebody had to."

Jason cocked his head back and laughed. "Man, I'd like to have seen that. It was ballsy. But how do you know that fucker didn't have a gun or a knife?"

My blood went a little cold when he said it. I didn't have a good answer for him and I couldn't stop thinking about Bess's would-be protector from the alley shadows. Obviously, the blood I'd seen on the pavement hadn't belonged to Zeke since Jason saw him just an hour ago without a scratch on him. So what the hell really happened out there?

"I know," I said. "It wasn't one of my finer moments on the common sense scale. But it sure as hell felt good. You should have seen the look on Zeke's face. I think he about pissed himself."

"Well, I for one think you deserve a damn medal. But, be careful, baby girl. I just wouldn't want to see you caught up in Dr. Bess's drama just for trying to be a good friend."

Jason leaned forward and kissed me on the forehead. He really was a big, damn teddy bear. "You want me to walk you out?" he asked.

"I'm good," I said. "I've got about three more files to transcribe and I'm outta here. You go. You need to get some sleep. I know you're at the mill tonight too. I don't know how you do it. You part vampire?"

Jason made the most ridiculous face, tucking his upper lip at the top of his front teeth. I burst out laughing.

"Seriously, though," he said. "Just watch your back, huh? I meant what I said about Zeke. I love Bess as much as you do, but I don't want to see you getting hurt because of her bad choices."

It was my turn to lean forward and kiss Jason on the top of his head. "I know. And I will. Now get gone. If you hurry home, you might get to spend twenty quality minutes with Michael before you fall asleep in your soup. Tell him I said hi and give him a kiss for me. We need to have a cookout again soon. My place. I know how you two love slumming in my trailer park."

Jason gave me another goofy grin as he got up to leave. He sang off key all the way down the hall before the back door shut and muffled his voice.

Alone again, my mind drifted back to this morning's events. Jason had a point. Confronting Zeke might have saved Bess, at least temporarily, but there was no question I was on his radar now. I'd never backed down from a bully, and I wasn't planning to start now. Still, I grabbed the baseball bat and carried it with me out to my car later that night.

———

The next morning, I lingered at the curb behind the clinic on my way in. The pool of blood I'd spotted had dried there. That same feeling of unease crawled up my back, as if I were being watched. I straightened and looked over my shoulder. There was no one there. There hadn't been the night before either.

Still, something had been nagging me since the episode with Zeke. That loser at least had the decency to stay away this morning. Dr. Bess drove in by herself. She was bright and cheery, pretending like everything was perfectly normal. She was always like that after a bad fight with Zeke. I had no doubt if I cornered her and lifted her hair off her collar, I'd see bruises there. Or maybe she hid them beneath her long-sleeved shirt. Bess Kennedy had become a master of deception. Except everyone who knew her best was no longer fooled. A part of me could understand why her family had given up on her. But, it made me feel even more sorry for her. Zeke Redmond had succeeded in isolating her from the people who cared about her the most.

I didn't ask her about Zeke because I didn't want to hear another lie. So, we went about our day pretending. Like always. For her part, Bess managed to avoid me as much as she could. She had three spay surgeries scheduled and a whole slew of appointments in the afternoon. It meant I'd be staying late again dealing with transcriptions.

"I don't know why you enable her like that." Tina, Bess's intern, hovered at my shoulder while I worked on the latest batch of bloodwork on tomorrow's admissions.

Tina had been at the clinic for the shortest amount of time. She was quick, smart, and abrasive. In other words, she was a lot like me.

"Pray tell, what do you mean, my child?" I said, raising a wry eyebrow in Tina's direction.

"This." Tina flipped the pages of Bess's yellow notepad. "It's the twenty-first century. She should learn how to use a fucking computer."

"She knows how to use a computer," I said. "It's just her mind works better on pen and paper. And she doesn't *need* to use the computer because she has people like you and me to transcribe this stuff for her."

"Aren't you sick of it, though?" Tina said. She helped herself to Bess's desk, propping her feet on top of it. "I mean, it's so menial."

"Shit flows down, baby girl," I said, borrowing a phrase from Jason.

"Not for long," Tina said. "I've got six more weeks and I am out of this backwoods town. I don't know how you can stand it."

I gritted my teeth. Tina was young, I reminded myself. In her third year of veterinary school, she'd be eligible to pass her boards in one more year. God, I envied her. Like Bess, she had someone else to carry her water and pay her bills for her. Me? It was going take me at least three more years to save up just one semester. At this rate, I'd get my D.V.M. the year before I was eligible to retire.

Mercifully, Tina got up and bounced to another part of the office before she could piss me off any further. I put my own foot up on the desk. My eyes were drawn to the splash of dried blood staining my left tennis shoe. I'd forgotten about it yesterday. When I closed my eyes, I could see Zeke in the alley with the mystery man.

I hadn't imagined it. I'd seen a flash of silver. He doubled over in shock or pain. I'd *heard* flesh tearing, hadn't I? But he'd moved so fast after that, he couldn't have been hurt like I thought he was. Except for all the blood.

When I finished the last of Bess's notes, I powered down the computer and grabbed my purse from a hook by the door. Once again, I was the first one in and last one out. Tina hadn't even bothered with a friendly goodbye before she left for the day.

I was just about to lock up the lab when the sound of metal crashing to the floor sent fear racing through me.

"Tina?" I clutched my purse in front of me. My heart pounded inside my chest. Something fell over in the back room. I could have dismissed it as one of our overnight patients knocking over a water dish, except I knew we were vacant tonight. Tina had discharged the last one, a yellow labrador, over an hour ago.

"God, I'm losing my mind," I told myself. It was just the stuff with Zeke shuffling my cornflakes.

I put a hesitant hand on the door then pushed it open. The room was quiet and dark, not a tray out of place. Still, the hair prickled on the back of my neck as if someone had just been in here. I checked the cabinet doors. We kept the more potent medication locked up back here. The first four cabinets were locked tight. The fifth gave way when I pulled the latch.

"What the hell?" Jason must have gotten sloppy. I locked the door and tested it one last time before heading out. I had made it through the back door. If I'd just kept on going into the cool night air, everything might have gone differently. But, I didn't. Instead, I stopped near the alley. The familiar scent of blood hit my nostrils. A shadow in the corner moved and took shape. No. It wasn't possible. I took two staggering steps sideways and there he was.

Mr. Cigarette Model from the other night.

He stood in the shadows by the dumpster right where I'd seen him the morning before. He froze, eyes flashing. He was just as tall as I remembered with those smoldering eyes. His fingers closed around my wrists as I got to him. Heat seared through me, making me weak in the knees. He stared at me with eyes. Those eyes. They were an impossible color. Glinting gold with pupils far too big to be normal.

My own traveled down his rock solid chest beneath his taut t-shirt. There was a large, jagged hole at the front of it, and the edges were caked with dried blood.

"My God!" I went to him, unthinking. "You *are* hurt!"

THREE

LIAM

I let her find me. Later, I might tell myself it was an accident, that I'd heard the back door close and just wanted to be sure she was safe. The rest of my crew might even believe me, but I'd know it was a lie.

Back in the clinic, I could have caught the metal instrument tray before it hit the ground easily. She never would have heard a thing. But, I didn't. It landed with a loud bang and spun before it came to rest beneath the examination table. I pressed my back against the wall, keeping to the shadows again, but knew it wouldn't make me invisible. That's a power I didn't have. I got out of the clinic before she saw me, but now she knew someone had been there.

In the alley now, Molly stared at me, her eyes wide. I half expected her to be carrying the baseball bat. Instead, she drew me into the light. I straightened my back, rising to my full height. There was nothing I could say to her that could explain what I was doing there. In just a fraction of a second, I took in everything about her.

She wore maroon scrubs. *Molly Ravary.* Her name tag hung crooked over her right breast. The vee of her shirt dipped low enough that I could see the pink strap of the tank top she wore beneath it. Like yesterday, she had her dark hair pulled back in a messy ponytail with her straight-cut bangs hanging into her eyes.

In the end, I didn't have to explain anything. It was Molly herself who sought out logic where there was none.

"My God," she said, bravely moving toward me. "You *are* hurt. Let me help you."

The wolf stirred beneath my skin as her scent filled me. She smelled clean, sweet, female. But there was an undercurrent of fear skittering across her skin. Of course there was. That was smart. But, it didn't stop her from coming to me.

"Come with me," she said, fumbling for the keys to the clinic door. I should have turned and left. I could move so quickly she might tell herself she'd imagined it all. I was just a trick of the shadows. I didn't though. Instead, I followed her. We walked straight back to one of the examination rooms.

She grabbed a wad of gauze from the counter beside her and made a circular motion with her hand, pointing to my chest.

Puzzled, I looked down. My t-shirt was torn across the abdomen. In the day since confronting Zeke, I'd forgotten about it. He'd cut a jagged gash through the fabric; the edges of it were rimmed with dried blood. But, the wound he'd made had healed within an hour after the knife went in. To someone like Molly, that would be impossible.

I turned sideways, dodging Molly's touch before she got to me. "What? Oh. I think it's okay."

"Is that why you're here?" she asked, her nose wrinkling. She had curious dark eyes that searched my face.

My eyes flicked to the medication now locked up behind her. I'd had just enough time to stash the vials and bottles I stole behind the dumpster. I could move so quickly, she'd never even see me pick them up if she walked beside me out there. What would she think of me when she figured out what was missing?

"Is she all right?" I asked, figuring it was time to at least to attempt to cover up the real reason I was here. "Your boss. I thought I'd come back and check. That guy yesterday seemed pretty serious about hurting her."

Molly's face softened, but still, she kept glancing toward my stomach and the wound she thought I bore.

"I'm glad you did," she said. "I wanted to thank you. On Bess's behalf, I mean. As far as I know she's okay. But, she's Bess. She's hell bent on staying with that loser for the time being."

"She's lucky to have a friend like you," I said. "But you should be careful. Guys like that are more dangerous than you think."

No sooner had I said it before every protective instinct inside of me flared. If I hadn't been there, he could have hurt Molly. The knife he'd stuck in my gut might have killed a normal man. A vision flashed through my mind of that dull blade sinking into Molly's stomach, just below her ribcage. Good old Zeke must have been a hunter. He knew how to make it fatal. I coughed to cover the growl that erupted from my throat. Casting my eyes down, I didn't want Molly to see anything strange.

Down, wolf. This girl is safe, for now.

"Thanks," she said, advancing. "Now let me take a look at that cut. Did you see a doctor yesterday?"

I could have stopped her. It would have taken nothing. Just a turn of my shoulder, a step back. But, I stayed rooted to my spot as Molly reached for the hem of my tattered t-shirt and lifted it. Her eyes widened at what she saw. There was no wound. Not so much as a scratch. Just a jagged hole in the fabric.

"There's dried blood." she said. "I *saw* him do something to you. It happened so fast I thought maybe I was seeing things. Was I? Did he cut you?"

I closed my fingers around hers, intending to draw her away from me. The minute our skin touched, heat spread from my core, rocketing up my spine. My knees went weak for an instant and my vision darkened. The wolf awakened.

Beneath my thumb, I felt Molly's pulse flutter. Her own eyes flashed with a dark knowledge she couldn't possibly understand. Not yet.

She should have jerked away from me. Any normal woman would have. Hell, any normal woman might have screamed bloody murder at finding a dark stranger lurking in the back alley with no good explanation for being there. Why the hell didn't she?

"You're not okay," she said, her voice breathless. She did pull her hand from mine. But, she immediately put two fingers beneath my jaw, feeling for a pulse. She closed her eyes and listened.

My heart hammered inside of my chest, sending thunder from me to her. Molly's eyes snapped open. I was just as shocked at that moment as she was. I *knew* what it must have felt like for her. She'd been trying to read my pulse. Oh, she felt it all right, but it came pouring from me and into her. She stepped away.

"You should sit down," she said. "Hell, you should be in the emergency room. You feel like you're about to have a heart attack."

Then, her eyes changed. New realization dawned in them as she looked from me to the medication cabinet behind her.

"Wait," I said.

"Is that why you're here?" she asked, taking two steps back and crossing her arms in front of her. "For that?"

Molly put a hand flat on the cabinet and looked at me with new skepticism. "Your pulse is thready. You're diaphoretic. What are you on?"

"I'm not on anything."

She kept one eye on me then reached back. A lab coat and stethoscope hung on a hook against the wall. She stuck it in her ears and came to me.

"Wait," I said.

Molly pulled up my shirt and pressed the flat end of the scope in the center of my chest. She winced as the strong beat of my heart filled her ears, overwhelming her.

"You're not a doctor," I said, pulling her scope away. She held onto the end of my shirt with one hand. With the other, she smoothed her fingers over the space above my bellybutton where the shirt had been torn. A day ago, Zeke's knife had torn through my flesh. Now, the skin was smooth and tanned. Molly's eyes flicked to mine as she felt the solid, hard muscles of my abdomen. She looked up and up, her gaze resting on the large tattoo I had on my upper chest.

The wolf seemed to swell inside of me, aching to get out. I was hungry. Hungry for her.

"What is that?" she asked, growing even bolder. She pressed her palm against the dark, howling wolf's head inked at the center of my chest. Great wings spanned beneath him stretching almost to my shoulders. At their juncture, were two crossed daggers.

I caught Molly's wrist and pulled her hand away. It was as if I couldn't stand to have her touching me. Or rather, I couldn't stand to have her *only* touch me with her fingers. My need to kiss her, to pull her to me burned through me. She had to have felt it. I knew her own pulse rose to match mine. She couldn't possibly understand what it meant.

It was becoming more dangerous for me to stay here by the minute. The more Molly's presence called to my wolf, the easier it would be for others to track me.

"What do you need?" she asked, finally stepping away from me. Her proximity to me was sending her body haywire. Her forehead glistened with sweat. Her breasts heaved as she tried to catch her breath.

"Drugs? Food? Do you have a place to stay tonight?"

God. She thought I was some junkie. She thought I was homeless. I suppose she was half right.

"I suppose that's what you would think," I said. Twice she'd found me lurking in the shadows by the clinic. Of course she'd assume I was after the drugs.

She was right, of course. But not for the reason she thought.

"I told you," I lied. "I just wanted to make sure you and your friend were okay. That asshole yesterday is going to hurt her at some point. Badly. She won't always have you or me to come out of the shadows and step in. Have you told her that?"

"Of course I have. Everyone has. She won't call the police. When they come, she won't press charges. And you don't have to lecture me about Zeke. I know what he's capable of."

I rose to my full height, towering over her. "No," I said, my voice dropping low. "You have no idea what he's capable of." I did. I felt Zeke's murderous rage coming off of him in waves. It permeated his every pore.

"You shouldn't be here," Molly said, taking a cautious step away from me. I'd scared her.

I drank in every detail of her. Sweat beaded in the hollow of her throat. She swallowed hard, then licked her lips, her quick, pink tongue darting out.

"I know," I said.

"But you need something from me. This isn't just because of Zeke. I've never seen you around here before. You're not...you don't have a patient at this clinic. What's your name?"

I should leave. I could move so quickly I'd be nothing more than a blur of motion. There was a chance Molly would convince herself she'd imagined the whole thing. That would have been the smartest play. Except, I felt anything but smart around her. I felt feral.

"Liam," I said. "Liam McConnell. And you're right, you haven't seen me around before."

"You should go," she said. I knew she had to be thinking about how quickly she could get to her baseball bat. I knew it wouldn't have mattered if she had the thing in her hands. On some preternatural level, so did she. But, it wasn't fear I sensed from her. Oh, no. It was desire.

"You're right," I answered. "I should go. I'm just glad you're all right."

Molly nodded. "I am too, Liam. I mean, I'm glad that you're all right. I guess I'd only been imagining things."

"I guess so."

I moved around her, heading for the door. Molly backed up, putting her hands behind her on the counter. Her posture made her breasts thrust forward and my eyes were drawn there. I found myself wanting desperately to run my hands beneath her scrub top and feel the weight of her breasts in my hands. Or maybe I could steal just one kiss.

In the end, I had no choice but to keep on walking. Molly stayed cemented to her spot, though I could feel her hot breath at my back as I headed out the door. Her tiny, fluttering pulse echoed through me, and I knew she could feel the thunder of mine heating her blood.

I headed out into the night. It wasn't safe here. There were shifters to the north, closing in fast. I'd been careless for the second time in a row where Molly was concerned. Stupid. So stupid. At least I'd managed to get what I came for. In a move so quick Molly couldn't process it. I grabbed the things I stole and stuffed them into my pocket.

"Liam?" Molly's voice cut through me as sharp as Zeke's knife. I wanted to turn and go to her, but then she'd see. I couldn't keep the wolf at bay for a second longer. If I faced her, she'd see my eyes and wouldn't be able to deny what I was.

"Wait," she called again. I curled my fists, letting my sharp claws out just enough to draw blood in the well of my palm. Now, I had no choice but to put as much distance between myself and the town as I could. The patrols would be on me in minutes if I stayed in one place. If the Alpha's general found me, I'd be done for.

As a full moon rose, I headed for the safety of the woods as Molly called my name behind me. Her voice reached me, whispering on the wind. It seemed to hover around me in the ether, tethering me to her.

Molly.

FOUR

LIAM

Molly. With each beat of my heart, I felt closer to her even as I ran further away. It was so stupid of me to think I could be near her without it affecting me like this. I kept her name close, guarding it with my heart like a secret.

Something else rose within me alongside my burning desire for Molly. It was dark, dangerous. It sucked the air from my lungs. As I ran at top speed, sweat poured down my back. God, I ached to shift. My wolf pulled at me, making my muscles clench and my bones rattle.

So close. I was so close. I hit the tree line. Dead leaves crackled beneath my feet as I followed the west trails. Tall poplars hid the moon. Ahead of me, a doe with her twin fawns darted out of my path. They had nothing to fear. I wasn't here for them tonight.

I could feel the underground spring bubbling beneath my feet as the woods grew denser. With each beat of my heart, it got harder to breathe. They were coming. I'd been too careless. Two nights in a row in town. Both times I'd come too close to letting the wolf out. They knew. They could sense me. They were closing in.

God. I had to be quicker. If they figured out I'd headed for Mammoth Forest, they would follow. I would die before I led them to the caves.

To the east, a chorus of howls rose, sending a chill down my spine. There was no more time. Another few seconds, and the patrolling shifters would pinpoint my location. Then, everything we'd worked and died for would be lost. It would all be my fault.

I could feel the safe spaces beneath my feet, snaking out deep underground. Dark passageways and caverns spiraling down and down for hundreds of miles. Humans would never find them; only shifters could. If the Chief Pack ever realized we hid there, everything I'd sacrificed would be for nothing. There was already a bounty on my head.

No human would ever be able to find the hole in the ground that led to the caves. There were times that even I lost sight of it. Not tonight though. Tonight, every life that mattered to me depended on me getting there in time.

I did.

Sliding to a halt, I kicked leaves up on either side of me as I dove for the cave opening. My shoulder popped as I hit it on the rocky outgrowth on the other side. Without even thinking, I shoved it back into joint.

To be safe, I piled dirt behind me, concealing the small entrance even more. In near pitch darkness, I felt along the cool rock walls until I felt the curve. Pressing my back against the wall, I slid into the antechamber. There, my breathing eased. The howls had faded to nothing. My heartbeat was my own again. I was safe.

A torch flared in front of me, and two cool green eyes hovered for a moment in the darkness then stepped into the light.

"You're late," Keara said. She held the torch in front of her and rested her other hand on her hip.

She wasn't much bigger than Molly at five feet two. Keara's hair matched the blazing torch she held. She thrust it before her so she could see me better. She had only human eyes, after all. The rest of us didn't need the light to see down here.

"Sorry," I said. "I ran into a little trouble."

Keara's eyes narrowed. She looked behind her. Jagger moved out of the shadows. His dark hair shone beneath the torchlight. Further into the cave, we had a system of LED lights set up. But here, so close to the mouth, it was better to keep things natural.

"You okay?" Jagger asked. He towered over his wife. The heat coming off them was palpable. Jagger could scarcely go five minutes without touching Keara in some small way. Now, he held a protective hand at the small of her back.

"Come on," he said. "The others have been bouncing off the walls waiting for some news from you."

Nodding, I followed them. Guilt washed over me with each step I took. For his part, Jagger didn't ask me any questions as we moved deeper into the cave system. He reached back and took Keara's hand. Part of the trail grew treacherous as we passed a narrow ridge beside a hundred foot drop.

It took a full ten minutes to get to the deepest part of our encampment. Keara hit a switch drilled into the wall, turning on the string of LED lights along the floor. The others had gathered in a large antechamber. Stalagmites jutted from the floor. Between them, we'd set up cots and tents. Any one of us would have preferred to sleep in the open air, but it had grown too risky. The humans who stayed with us could, but for the five shifters that formed the core of our group, the danger of drawing the Chief Pack's shifter patrols was far too great.

Jagger leaned down to kiss Keara before moving away from her. Mac, Gunnar, and Payne stepped out of the shadows. It was just the five of us here plus Keara at the moment. When we could, we housed human and shifter refugees and tried to help them cross the border and get free of the Chief Pack. For the five of us though, it was far too dangerous to try. We'd been marked by the Chief Pack as their most wanted traitors. Even across the border they would come for us.

"Well?" Mac asked. His wolf eyes flashed silver, stirring my own beast. God. It had been three days since I'd last shifted. Some nights I thought I'd go mad from it. Mac, I knew, hadn't dared to shift in almost two weeks. My half-brother, Mac and I had different fathers. But, we shared the same auburn hair that turned steel-gray when we came into our wolves.

"I managed to get a few things," I said, grateful to at least be able to tell them that truth. "I was telling Jagger and Keara, I ran into a little bit of human trouble. Nothing I can't handle, but I'm going to have to go back to the clinic tomorrow. I got some painkillers, some of the antibiotics Keara wanted. There's more though. I'm going to have to go back for it."

"Shit," Payne said. He paced in front of the cots. He'd begged me to let him go on this run with me. We needed a steady supply of medicine. The vet clinic seemed safer than the hospitals and doctor's offices we'd tried. We couldn't do what we did without human help. Sometimes, that put them at risk. Sometimes they got hurt because of it. We were trying to stockpile medical supplies in case the worst happened. Unfortunately, it did often enough to cause worry.

I gave them the highlights of my encounter with Zeke the night before. "I'm sorry," I said. "I know I shouldn't have gotten involved. But, you should have seen this asshole. I think he was going to kill that vet."

I left Molly out of my story. Jagger, Payne, Mac, and Gunnar hung on my words. Each of them gave me growls of support from time to time, but none of them questioned the details. It was only

Keara who hung back, pursing her lips. It wasn't like her not to interrogate me just as much as the others did.

"You did what you had to do," Jagger said. He came to me, putting a strong hand on my shoulder. "Let's wait a few days, let the dust settle. Then, you can go back."

My heart hammered behind my ribcage. If anyone were going to sense a change in me, it would be Jagger. Just like Mac, Jagger and I were kin, after all, first cousins through our mothers. If it weren't for Jagger, I'd still be up there, held against my will by the Kentucky Chief Pack. I owed him for that and so much more. Still, I couldn't bring myself to tell him the complete truth about what I found at the Shadow Springs Veterinary Clinic. Because I knew, the moment I did, all hell would break loose.

"It's maybe a good thing," Gunnar said. "I mean, this doctor. She owes you one. At a minimum, maybe it means she'll look the other way if you have to break into the place and steal more meds."

"I thought of that," I said. "I still think it's better if you let me work an angle. I've only taken a few things. But, once they figure it out. We can't go back there. If I get cooperation on the inside, maybe we can solidify a reliable contact."

"That's dangerous," Keara said, narrowing her eyes as she walked closer to me. "The more people we bring in, the more danger they're in."

"I know that. Don't you think I know that? I've been *living* up there for the past few days. I know what the risks are."

Jagger's wolf simmered and growled. I took a step back and held up my hands in a conciliatory gesture. He knew I'd never in a million years do anything to hurt Keara. None of us would. But, she had been the one to press us for human help in the first place. She had grand designs about making this place a more sophisticated hideout and building a network of contacts above ground.

"I just need time," I said. "A few more days. Let me try to work it."

"You already have a contact in mind, don't you?" Keara said. God, for a human, she seemed more in tune to our moods than any shifter I ever knew. I loved it about her most of the time. Right now, it was damned annoying.

Jagger raised a brow. A smile lifted the corner of his mouth. I think he enjoyed it when Keara took me on.

"Yes," I said.

"Good," Jagger answered. The others quickly agreed with him. Keara's eyes narrowed even further. She came up to me.

"Just be careful, Liam," she said. "I may not be a shifter, but whatever happened up there is messing you up. I can smell it on you." She reached up and tweaked my nose.

FIVE

LIAM

I spent the next few days underground. After getting so close to Molly, my need to shift into my wolf was nearly unbearable. I tried to get my mind off it by helping Mac and Gunnar excavate a new tunnel we'd found branching off the main antechamber. Keara wanted to turn it into a makeshift infirmary in case we ever needed it. It was back-breaking work, shoveling out gravel and dirt. But, the rhythmic monotony of it helped calm my inner beast.

Payne had gone topside. He'd taken a tip that there was a wolf shifter friendly to our cause hiding out ten miles east of us. Those missions were always the most dangerous. Was it truly another shifter in need, or was it a spy for the Chief Pack? The safer thing to do was keep to ourselves. But, if we'd done that, we'd never have found Gunnar, or Payne.

We all had different reasons for going underground. Mine was family. When Jagger left, I went with him. As my half-brother, Mac came for me. He had another reason as well. Our mother had mated with two different shifters. Mac had me for a half-brother on her side. He also had a human half-sister on his father's side named Lena. Lena had disappeared. He believed she'd been taken somewhere for use by the Pack. He hoped someday to find her. Gunnar and Payne had also suffered under the rule of the Pack and lost people dear to them. Now, we had each other.

At the end of the workday, Jagger found me. I'd claimed a smaller antechamber that branched off the main conduit we used to go in and out of the caves. It was dark, quiet, and connected to the natural springs on the east side, giving me fresh, cool water whenever I needed it.

"You okay, man?" Jagger asked, his keen eyes flashing silver as he leaned against the cave entrance. I had lanterns, but I'd kept them off, preferring the dark solitude. It suited my mood.

"Yeah," I answered. I sat on a natural limestone ledge. It was probably two in the morning, but I couldn't sleep. Jagger and I weren't part of a pack, but he was blood. We were connected in other ways and he knew me well. I could fool the others, but never him or Mac.

"Ever since you got back from recon at that vet clinic, you've been off, man. Something you want to tell me about?"

"Not really," I said. "It just gets hard sometimes, you know?"

The air went still. Sometimes, when I closed my eyes and held my breath, this place felt like a tomb. No sound. No light. Just cool air and stillness. Most days, it helped to calm me. Today, I was agitated enough I felt like I could claw my way through the stone walls.

The truth was, of all of us, Jagger didn't know. He'd found his fated mate in Keara. In fact, she was the entire reason our motley band of resistance had formed in the first place. The Chief Alpha would never have sanctioned the match between them. No shifter in the state of Kentucky was allowed to freely choose their mate. Anyone who went against the Chief Pack faced swift execution if they were lucky. More likely, that wolf would be kept alive and tortured to send a message to any other man who thought about rebelling.

Jagger moved further into the room. He tread carefully, sensing the turmoil within me. In another time, in another place, we might both have been Alphas of our own packs. God, what would that be like? Having the freedom to choose our own mates, carve out our own territory, and finding a group of shifters loyal to us. I couldn't think it. I'd go mad if I dreamed it.

"How did you know?" I asked. The words just popped out of my head. It would have been smarter to just keep it to myself.

"Know what?" Jagger asked. He sat on the ledge next to me, resting his head against the stone wall.

"With Keara," I said, letting out a hard breath.

Jagger's low laughter bounced off the cave walls. "I can't really explain it. It just was. The minute I got near enough to scent her, everything just changed. She said it was like that for her too. She said it was like having a second heartbeat. Then just one, ours. You'll know it when it happens. It just comes over you, hitting you like a thunderbolt, and all of a sudden you can't imagine what your life was like before. There's no doubt. No question. There's just her. A craving."

Jagger's face changed. His eyes darkened and he frowned. He didn't have to tell me what bothered him. Jagger had committed the ultimate act of rebellion against the Chief Alpha. Mating with Keara was one thing. He'd also marked her as his own. It meant they were connected forever in an unbreakable bond. He'd claimed her. If they weren't careful, she could give birth to his son. His shifter son. He would be instantly marked for death from the Alpha the moment he drew breath.

My cousin Jagger was the most hunted shifter in all of Kentucky next to me. If he was ever caught, he'd face brutal torture for the rest of his days. He'd become a trophy for the Chief Alpha. I shuddered just to think of it.

"I know I was selfish," he said. "And every single day I wonder if Keara and you wouldn't be better off if I'd just tried to cross the border alone."

"Don't say that," I said. "Don't even think that. God. Jagger...I'll admit, when you first came to me with what you'd done, I was angry. It seemed so reckless. But, if you hadn't, I know I would have tried to find a way to break away by myself. You were brave before I was. You just gave me the final push I needed to do what was already in my heart."

Jagger's eyes flicked to mine. "You sure about that, Liam? I mean, look at us. Look at how we have to live. If we hadn't found this place, we'd be dead by now, or worse. As it is, we're living underground. You think I don't worry every single day about how long we can survive here? What kind of life is this for Keara? For our family if we ever dare to have one?"

"We've all made the only choices we could," I said. It was in me to say so much more. I knew I should tell him about Molly. Our entire group relied on one another for survival. If we started keeping secrets, it could put everyone at risk.

"Maybe," Jagger said. "But, I wonder."

"What?"

Jagger shrugged. He bounced his head gently against the wall. "It's just...I feel them getting closer. Don't you?"

My blood turned to ice. I wished I could tell Jagger he was imagining things. We were safe enough down here. Miles underground, the Chief Pack hadn't yet been able to sense us. The Alpha was powerful and his minions well-trained, but even their telepathy couldn't pierce that mile of stone between us. It entombed us, but it also protected us. If they ever found out we were hiding down here, that would be another story.

But, Jagger was right. Each time I went topside I could feel the pull of the Chief Pack getting stronger. It acted on me like a drug. The urge to submit seemed like the easier choice. No more pain. No more torture. I could stop thinking and just be. That was the seduction of the Alpha's power.

"Come on, man," I said. I knew Jagger had come in here to see if I was all right. The tables had turned. "We've come this far. I'm going to go back up there tomorrow. I'll get the rest of the medical supplies we need. Somehow."

"Maybe it's too risky," he said. "I know Keara wants all of it so we can be ready for anything. I don't want you going up there if you don't feel safe."

I laughed. "Right. And if I don't go, you know Keara will. You want that instead?"

I'd meant it as a lighthearted comment, but Jagger's eyes grew hard. My breath went out of me in a whoosh as I realized the insensitivity of my remark. Keara would be defenseless without us. When Jagger marked her, he was only serving a thousand years' worth of instinct. They were fated. He was *supposed* to be with her. But, her connection to him made her a weapon against him if they ever found her. She'd never be able to withstand the interrogation from the Chief Pack. Plus, if she were ever captured, I knew we'd lose Jagger too. At the same time it strengthened him, claiming Keara had opened up an Achilles' heel that put us all at risk.

"Enough!" The voice came from down the corridor. Keara stepped into view. Her smile was soft, but her eyes hardened as she looked at Jagger.

"How long have you been standing there, woman?" Jagger smiled. It was a bullshit question. Jagger could sense Keara's whereabouts from miles away. They shared a telepathic link. He would forever know when Keara was in danger. Her pain was his pain. A cold shudder went through me as I was again reminded how dangerous that could be if Keara was ever captured.

Jagger had done what he had to, but he was right it put us all at risk. My mind drifted back to Molly and the cold shudder gave way to thrilling heat. My heart beat faster as I closed my eyes and conjured her. She stood strong and fierce with those wide, brown eyes.

I craved her. Pure and simple.

"Liam?" My eyes snapped open. Keara had come into the room. Jagger rose and stood shoulder to shoulder with her. He put a protective arm around her waist and drew her to him. They were one, inseparable. As big a risk as she was, I knew Jagger would die a thousand times over just to be with her. His words washed over me.

You'll know it when it happens. It just comes over you, hitting you like a thunderbolt, and all of a sudden you can't imagine what your life was like before. There's no doubt. No question. There's just her. A craving.

God, yes. A craving. Molly.

"So you're going back up there tomorrow?" she asked. Of course she'd overheard everything Jagger and I said.

"What? Yeah. Tomorrow."

"Good," Keara said. She broke away from Jagger and came to me. She put the back of her hand to my forehead and her eyes narrowed with concern.

I pulled away, gently guiding her hand from me. "Quit fussing," I said.

"Hmm. You're running hotter than usual, Liam. Just be extra careful. Don't take any unnecessary risks. We need the meds, but we need you more. Got it?"

Jagger came to her, giving her a playful swat on her ass. Keara's eyes flashed with dark lust. My own wolf stirred. It was hard to be around them sometimes. As much as we loved Jagger and Keara both, it reminded the rest of us what we were missing. Normally, I could distract myself with a run or hard labor. Now, my inner wolf blazed inside of me. One thought pounded through me in a constant drumbeat.

Molly. Molly. Molly.

"Got it," I said, my voice cracking. "No unnecessary risks."

I couldn't take being this close to them another second. Jagger would easily sense the change in me. I brushed past them, heading out for the main rotunda. From there, I'd go back down the corridor and dig. My whole body vibrated with the anticipation of seeing Molly again tomorrow.

Maybe I'd imagined the whole thing. We were all so keyed up with the Chief Pack growing stronger. It had to be that. The alternative was unthinkable. Except, all I could *do* was think about it.

Molly meant something. I craved her. Her scent hit me like a thunderbolt. She wasn't just some girl. She was mine. God help us all.

SIX

MOLLY

For the third night in a row, I woke tangled in the bedsheets, dripping with sweat. "The hell?"

My heart raced as I threw the sheets to the floor and slid out of bed. Mid-September and a cool breeze floated through my open window. Crickets chirped outside and I went to the front door. Two trailers down from me, I could hear soft laughter and music playing. My neighbor, Lisa Ray, was always looking for her next hookup. More often than not, she chose guys who would get along great with Zeke Redmund.

A full moon hung low in the sky and the bullfrogs were out. Shady Acres sat nestled in the valley with a scenic view of Mammoth Forest in the distance. Well, scenic if you could over-look the few dozen rows of beat up trailers along the way. Shady Acres was aptly named. How could I *not* rent a lot here?

Lisa's laughter rose and I heard her feign a protest when her guy of the night moved in on her. Then, her screen door slammed and they took their party inside.

I grabbed a hoodie from the couch and stepped outside. Barefoot and still in my pajamas, I fit right in with the dress code around here. My hair whipped around my face as I headed up the small path to the courtyard. It was empty this time of night. On a Wednesday, that wasn't unusual. When the weekend came around, this place had a constant campfire going up until almost Thanksgiving.

Gathering my sweatshirt tighter around me, I looked toward the woods. Something skittered along my spine and the chill I'd felt seemed to blossom into a familiar warmth that I couldn't quite place. For about the dozenth time in the last week, I felt like someone was watching me. Instead of unsettling me, excitement thrummed through me. I wasn't myself.

"Everything okay, Molly?" Lisa poked her head out her front door.

"I'm good." I waved at her. A hand slid around her shoulders, pulling her back. Lisa playfully slapped at it and gave me knowing wink.

"Have fun, Lisa," I called out. "Don't worry about little old me."

Lisa made a joke about what not to do if her trailer was rocking. I bit back a retort. Hell, if we lived by that rule, no one would ever visit Lisa. I headed back down the little trail toward my place. Still, I felt eyes on me. When I looked toward the woods, everything seemed dark, still, and normal. It wasn't though. It hadn't been for days. Ever since…

When I closed my eyes, I saw Liam McConnell's face swimming in front of me. I swear, if I hugged myself I could almost smell him. He had a clean, warm, masculine scent. There was something woodsy about it, and I wondered what he did for a living. God, who was I kidding? Liam McConnell probably didn't do anything at all. He had that desperate look about him I'd seen a hundred times. He could pretend all he wanted, but he'd come to the clinic looking for meds. There was no point in him trying to hide it. Not for a second. Shadow Springs was a small-ass town. I'd never seen him before. And his clothes had been dirty and torn. He was homeless. No question about it. Homeless and looking for a fix. And he was far gone enough to think he could find what he needed from a vet. God, why couldn't I get him out of my mind? My blood heated just imagining the feel of his strong arms around me. It was crazy. *I* felt like I was going crazy. This wasn't the kind of thing that usually stirred me up. Homeless junkie, that was more Lisa's style.

When I reached my trailer, I still couldn't go inside. There was something out there. I should have been afraid. I should have marched right back inside and slammed the door. I didn't. Instead, I walked around the back. My lot abutted the edge of the woods. When I bought it, I thought it would give me some privacy. It did, but the lots were still pretty tightly packed. It wasn't much, but it was all mine. My double-wide was paid in full. All I owed was lot rent. I was beholden to nothing and no one.

I ventured closer to the edge of the woods. Mammoth Forest stretched for miles in all directions. Just a little ways up the inter-state, this land turned into Mammoth Cave National Park. Living as close as I did, I'd only ever gone to the caves a few times as a kid. My father last took me when I was eleven years old the summer before he died. It had been just the two of us. Mama refused, citing severe claustrophobia. Daddy, on the other hand, loved it there. He'd worked as a park ranger through college before he met my mother and everything changed.

Lois Ravary had been a knockout in her day. She'd had her pick of a hundred men, but she'd chosen Daddy. A fact she reminded him of every day of their miserable marriage. He could never keep her happy. No one could. My mother had untreated bipolar disorder. When she was up, my childhood had been an adventure. When she was down, we all paid. Daddy kept her level as well as he could. When he was gone, it had fallen to me. I got out as soon as I could. She still hated me for it, and we hadn't talked in years.

Nope. I didn't mind living in my trailer park. I was free and it made me feel close to my father somehow. I knew the cave system probably stretched below my very feet.

A howl rose in the distance. My heartbeat tripped. To my trained ear, that didn't sound like a coyote. If I didn't know better, I'd say it was a wolf. The chill came back and I zipped my hoodie. The howl rose one more time as I turned to step back inside.

———

We were slammed the next day. Bess had back-to-back surgeries. She'd walked in sporting an angry bruise on her upper arm. Jason and I gave her the same look. Bess tried to pull a sweater on before we saw, but it was no good. Today though, I didn't have the energy to get into it with her. I'd heard that plaintive howl four more times before I finally fell into a fitful sleep the night before. Now, I couldn't wait to get home and get to bed.

When I finished running labs for Bess, she found me in the break-room. Biting her lip, she leaned against the door. I knew what she was here to say and I decided to make it easy on her for once.

"Bess," I said. "I get it. Your shit is none of my business. You already know what I think, so let's just not do this. Save us both the aggravation. But, I'm also not going to pretend I didn't see your arm."

"I kicked him out," she said, spitting it out in a gushing breath.

I reared back. This was new. "You did what?"

"It's over, Molly. Last straw. I called my brothers and they helped me throw Zeke's things to the curb. They're over at my place right now changing the locks. I thought you'd like to know."

I beamed, going to her. I wanted to hug her, but Bess Kennedy seemed so frail. She'd been broken so many times. But, she was still here, standing as tall and strong as she could. I was proud of her, I just hoped she'd stick to her guns this time. I decided not to mention that we'd all heard this story from her before.

"I'm glad. You did the right thing, Bess. You know you can call me if you ever need anything. Shady Acres isn't much, but I've got a nice view of the woods. You can crash at my place if you want to get away."

"Thanks," Bess said, smoothing her lab coat. "I think it's going to be all right for now though. I think Zeke knows I mean it."

"Well, if that's true, then I'm glad. You deserve better, Bess. We all think so. You're pretty. You're young. More importantly, you're smart. You could have any man you want. Or, better still, you don't need one."

Bess dropped her head so her hair fell over her eyes. I could never understand how a woman as accomplished as Bess Kennedy was could have so little self-esteem. I think she'd been hurt by men her entire life.

"I'm not like you," Bess said, lifting her head just enough so that her hair fell away.

"What do you mean?"

"Oh, come on, Molly. You're so sure of yourself. You'd never let anyone mess with you. You have all the answers."

Coming from anyone else, her last comment might have seemed like an insult. I knew she meant it as a compliment. "Oh, I don't know about that. I think maybe I just do a better job faking it than you do."

"Well, you're always asking me what I want. What about you? What do you want? You can't want to spend your life squeezing anal glands and trimming corgi toenails, do you? When are you going to go back to school?"

A tone came over the intercom. After a few seconds of static, Jason's voice filled the room. "Molly, Misty's in exam two for you."

I had to laugh at that. Misty was a hundred and forty pound golden retriever. She was probably here for her glands and nails. Bess's smile widened. I hit the button on the wall. "Tell Misty and Beau I'll be there in three minutes."

"Next year," I answered Bess's question. She gave me a wry smile.

"You've been saying that for two years now. You need to step up your timetable. You'll make a great vet. I should know. Plus, I don't want to run this place by myself. I wouldn't mind having a partner."

My pulse skyrocketed. It got a little hard to breathe. I'd never really let myself think that far ahead. "Are you serious?"

"Yes," she answered. "You're right. I need a life too. A better one. Time off would be heaven. Think about it at least."

I wanted to hug her. Hell, I wanted to kiss her. Except, that familiar pit formed in my stomach. The issue was money. I just straight up didn't have it right now. Getting a D.V.M. simply cost too much. I had just managed to scrape by enough money to put myself through vet tech school. Anything more was just a pipe dream.

"Of course, if I can't get things straightened out around here, there won't be much of a practice to share."

"What do you mean?" I asked. We were booked solid for the next three months.

Bess brushed a hair from her face. "I'm sorry to dump all of this stuff on you, but I'm going to need you to help me check inventory later. I think I've miscounted. There were some things missing from one of the medicine cabinets this morning. I'm sure it's my mistake. We both know my bookkeeping is terrible."

My heart lurched. There were meds missing. I'd been the last man out and I could have sworn I heard something in the back room. I'd brushed it off as nothing. Liam had pretty much drowned out all reason from my head. When I closed my eyes, I could feel the warmth of his hands over me. But there had been something wrong with him too. His heart beat too fast. His color was strange.

"Molly? What're you thinking?"

"What? Oh. No. Nothing. But, yes. I can help you cross check the inventory. I'm sure it's just a transposed number or something."

Now, I was covering. I knew in my heart if we had missing medication, Liam McConnell might have something to do with it. And yet, there I was protecting him, ready to make excuses just like Bess did with Zeke. What the hell had gotten into me?

I heard a howl down the hall. For a moment, my heart stopped, thinking about the wolf I'd heard last night. But, it was just Misty. Her howl saved me from having to make any more excuses.

"You better get on that," Bess said. "Call me if you need my help."

I patted her on the shoulder. "I got this. And thank you. You're a good friend."

"Right," Bess said. "You're a better one."

———

For once, I finished Bess's notes early. After discharging our last surgery patient, I was antsy to get out of the clinic. In her typical scatterbrained fashion, Bess had forgotten all about the inventory discrepancy she wanted me to check. I'd done it anyway though. Bess had been right. We were missing several bottles of broad spectrum antibiotics. That in and of itself might not have caused me much alarm. But, we were also missing several bottles of Tramadol. It was one of the most potent pain relievers we kept in stock, reserved mostly for our surgical patients as we sent them home with their owners. I tried to push my suspicions out of my mind as it became time to clock out.

Jason had only worked a half day and Bess was already gone. Even though it was just past four and the sun still shone bright, I felt odd walking back to my car alone. That same sensation of eyes on me made the hair on the back of my neck stand on end.

I'd parked in my usual spot across the street. I clicked the locks. Tossing my bag into the front seat, something made me look back the clinic. I did a double take. There was movement to the right, behind the dumpster.

"What the bloody hell?" I hit the door locks again and walked back toward the building.

"Zeke, that better not be you." Even as I said it, it wasn't what I was really thinking. I tried the back door, double checking that I'd engaged the lock. It didn't budge.

There was nothing there, not so much as a stray cat. Sometimes, people would leave kittens or other wounded animals they didn't want in boxes by the back door. It happened more often than people would ever believe. We didn't have the resources to care for abandoned animals. Most of them were too sick to even be helped. Usually the best we could do was euthanize them. The kittens were the worst. We worked with a local shelter trying to rehome them, but far too many had tragic outcomes.

I looped around to the front door, holding my breath. Luckily, there was nothing on the porch step but the green welcome mat Bess kept there. Straightening, I turned back around and headed for my car.

I made it about halfway before turning one more time. I put a hand on the brick wall, peering around the alley.

"You might as well come out," I said. "I know you're back there. You suck at hiding."

The wind shifted, blowing my hair back. Heat shot straight down my spine. A pulse pounded in my ears that didn't feel like my own. Impossible. You can't *hear* someone else's heartbeat like that. And yet, that's exactly what it felt like.

Then, Liam stepped out of the shadows. His eyes glinted in the setting sun, turning them gold. Except the sun was behind him.

He took three slow steps toward me and my heart dropped into my shoes. I took a step back. I had to get around him to get to my car. Instead, I stayed rooted to one spot, afraid to move, afraid to breathe.

He stopped just in front of me. A muscle jumped in his jaw as his eyes flicked over me, studying me. His features seemed to change as I looked at him just as intently. One moment, his eyes were blue; the next, they flashed gold. Impossible. I had to be seeing things. He wore fresh clothes at least. His t-shirt stretched taut over his hard muscles. I had the urge to touch him, running my fingers over his biceps and straight up to his shoulders. God, what was I thinking? I didn't know him. This was three times now I'd caught him lurking around the clinic looking for what...for me? I let out a hard breath. No, not for me. He was here to score. There could be no other explanation. I don't know why I just hadn't voiced my suspicions to Bess about who might have broken into the clinic. Why was I protecting him?

"I can't help you," I said, my voice cracking. "I don't know what you think you're going to get from me, but you should just go."

Liam nodded. His eyes darted back and forth. He seemed to be having just as much trouble breathing as I was. It was as if the air between us had grown thicker. His fingers twitched at his sides like he didn't know what to do with them. Like he was trying to keep himself from...from touching me. "I know what you did," I said. My heart was beating so loud between my ears I couldn't think straight. Every shred of common sense I had was telling me to run. Don't engage. I knew Liam was likely the one who'd broken into the clinic. He was dangerous. Even now, as he stood before me, I could see the signs. The sweat on his brow, his ashen color. He clenched his fists at his sides, but he couldn't hide the tremors. He was either in some serious drug withdrawal, or worse still, he'd taken something. God, he had to be seriously bad off if he'd resorted to stealing cat tranquilizers.

"Molly," he said, his voice barely sounding human.

He took a step toward me. I should run. I should scream. But, as I felt his body heat pouring off him in waves, my nerve endings ignited. If Liam was craving drugs, I was craving something else. Him.

I had my car keys in my hand. I stuck the jagged edge between my index and middle fingers, holding it out as a weapon.

"I'm not here to hurt you," Liam said, his eyes widening in shock. "God. I would never hurt you."

"You need help," I said. "I looked the other way before. I can't do it again. There's a free clinic about ten miles from here. You can catch the bus one block over. Go there. Get help."

Liam raised his hand and tore his fingers through his hair. He cast a glance over his shoulder. He was scared of something. What in God's name could scare someone as big and lethal-looking as Liam?

"It's not what you think," he said. "But you're right. I shouldn't have come back here. But, I had to see. I had to know if…"

"If what?"

Liam went incredibly still. The tremors stopped and he squared his shoulders. In one breath, he seemed to shake off the effects of whatever drug his body craved. Heat rose between us. Just as he seemed to be pulling himself together, I was falling apart. It started as warmth in my gut. It spread, dragging me forward. We stood only inches from each other, but it seemed too far. I wanted him to touch me. I wanted to inhale his scent and feel his strong arms around me.

"Liam?" I said, my throat dry as sandpaper.

The pounding in my chest steadied. Again, I had that strange sensation of hearing dual heartbeats. Liam's and mine. I was losing my mind.

"I'm sorry...I shouldn't have..."

He came to me. I felt frozen. I knew that everything else in my life would be separated between the moment before and the moment after.

It was such a simple gesture. Liam reached for me. He slid his fingers to the back of my neck, lacing them through my hair. His thumb brushed my cheek. The air went out of me in a whoosh. It was as if his fingertips ignited every pleasure center inside of me. My knees went weak. The throbbing pulse between my legs spread. My nipples hardened. The urge to kiss him burned through me.

"Liam," I gasped.

His eyes darted over me. His lips parted. I zeroed in on every detail of his face. Hard stubble shaded his square jaw. His earlobes reddened and his breath caressed my neck. A junkie, I told myself. He had to be. Except, when his eyes glinted, they held their stone-cold focus on mine. His head was clear. He was so close and yet, not close enough.

I don't know who moved first. I think it was him, but it might have been me. Before I knew what was happening, I tilted my head to the side and sank into him.

Then, Liam kissed me.

I closed my eyes and fireworks exploded behind them. Liam's touch seemed to short-circuit every sense in my body. It was as if I no longer existed alone inside myself. He was there. Consuming me at the same time he kindled a deep fire low in my core. God, I wanted. Naked lust poured through me. I couldn't control it. I knew in the deepest parts of me that if Liam wanted it, I would let him take me then and there. It was raw, primal, thunderous.

Liam broke away first. Whatever was happening inside of me, Liam had a similar reaction. The shudder came back and he took two halting steps backward. I thought my knees were weak, but it was Liam who dropped to the ground.

"Liam?"

He was on his hands and knees in the middle of the alley. His back contorted. At first, I thought he was going to have a seizure. I went to him, meaning to reach for his chin and bring his face up to meet my gaze.

"No," he said. His voice had turned guttural, filled with pain.

"I'm calling 911," I said. I'd dropped my purse on the ground. I reached for it now, fumbling to find my phone.

"No!" Liam said again, more forcefully this time. He turned from me as I reached for him a second time. It was as if he didn't want me to see his face.

A crack echoed through the alley. I recognized it as the sound of breaking bones. Liam threw his head back and I understood why he'd turned away.

It wasn't Liam anymore. His cheekbones were distorted, jutting out at wrong angles. He locked eyes with me, and that's when I screamed. Liam's had gone pure gold with the pupils larger than they should be. He didn't seem human, he seemed…canine.

The moment I thought it, Liam completed the transformation. He wasn't human anymore. His clothes tore violently from him. He lowered his head and gave one great shake. In Liam's place, the largest wolf I'd ever seen stood before me.

He was beautiful. His silvery coat glistened in the moonlight. He gazed at me with keen, intelligent eyes. The wolf's ears pricked back and he pawed the ground.

I should have been terrified. Maybe I was, but I realized with cold clarity that I had undergone a transformation nearly as shocking as Liam's in the same span of time. Things that should have scared me to death seemed to make perfect sense. One single thought repeated in my brain like a drumbeat.

What took you so long to find me?

I'd heard all the rumors told in hushed whispers all of my life. Shadow Springs held secrets outsiders could never understand. Some said real-life monsters prowled Mammoth Forest. But, those were just stories grownups told little ones to keep them from wandering off from campsites. Weren't they?

There were no such things as monsters. And yet, there were some people in this town others wouldn't stand up to no matter what. The mayor, the police chief, even the local weatherman.

Secrets. Lies. Whispers.

When I inhaled, the world was one thing. As I exhaled, it became something else, and all of the secrets and legends I'd tried to avoid came straight out of the shadows. I had no choice but to face them head on.

I reached for the wolf. Though my thoughts were calm, my body seemed to register the fear anyone else would have expected. My fingers trembled. Again, I had the sense that my life would be separated into chapters. Before Liam's touch, and after. I sank my fingers into the wolf's downy fur. He let out a soft wail and stomped his front paws on the ground.

"Liam," I whispered. Because, as impossible as it was, I knew he was in there. I knew he could understand me.

He let out a chuff and came to me, nuzzling the side of my leg. God, he was incredible. I admired the powerful muscles of his haunches as he extended his leg. He was far bigger than a normal wolf. He had to be more than two hundred pounds. The top of his head came almost to the center of my chest.

"Liam," I said again. He looked up at me, those golden eyes darting over me. I couldn't breathe. I couldn't move. Grasping for some semblance of reality, I tried to force my thoughts to something familiar and grounded.

Liam's coat was smooth and glossy. His eyes were bright and clear as he locked his gaze with mine. I slid my fingers across his chest, sinking them into his fur. There, near his elbow joint, I could feel his strong, steady pulse. My lips parted, quivering as I realized it thrummed in perfect synchrony with my own.

"I can't…" Gasping, I took a faltering step backward. Somehow, I managed to stay on my feet.

Liam's wolf pawed the ground again and took a tentative step toward me. Of course he couldn't speak, but something about his eyes transmitted a message loud and clear.

It's all right. I'm not ever going to hurt you.

I reached for him again; the impossible urge to press my cheek against his flank overwhelmed me. I wanted to run with him, be close to him, feel his powerful muscles beneath my fingers. Whatever else was happening, I knew I was in the presence of something magnificent.

Liam dropped his head, inviting me to approach. I bit my bottom lip and tried to drive out the sensation of feeling his heart beating along with mine. Less than an inch from making contact with him again, the air around us changed. The temperature dropped. Adrenaline rushed through me and my pulse thundered again. So did Liam's.

A high-pitched howl rent the air. It was coming from the east, toward the forest on the other side of town. Then, a second and third howl rose to join the first. Liam's eyes grew dark. He took three steps back, shaking his head. My ears weren't sensitive enough to hear what he did, but I felt his reaction in the cold chill inside my chest.

The howls grew more insistent. Liam turned in a circle. A low, threatening growl rumbled through him. His shoulders contorted and he flattened his body to the ground.

Magic like electricity crackled through the air. I felt it as pins and needles tingling throughout my entire body. But, it was coming from Liam. In no more than a second, he shifted again, rising tall on two muscular legs.

He was Liam, the man again. Except he was stark naked and towering in front of me. My jaw dropping, I took in the sight of him. His muscles rippled from his shoulders, down his taut abdomen, tapering to a vee at his hips. I couldn't help myself from staring at his impressive cock. It swung heavy as he took two steps toward me. An answering heat flared inside of me as if my body was trained to respond to his. I shook my head, trying to clear my thoughts.

Liam came to me as the distant howls drew closer.

"Molly," he said. His voice was low, threatening. "There's no time. Get in your car. Now. Drive away as fast as you can."

There was no time to ask even one of the thousand questions I had. Liam's wolf eyes flashed as the threat drew closer. God, I don't know how I knew, but I sensed it through Liam. There were three more wolves coming. And they were out for the kill.

"Run, Molly," Liam shouted as he rushed past me. Why he didn't shift back into his own wolf I couldn't understand. But, I felt the coming threat on a preternatural level. Fumbling for my keys again, I dashed to my car. I caught one last glimpse of Liam headed for the woods as I put the car in reverse. I laid rubber on the pavement as I slammed the stick into first gear and headed for home.

SEVEN

LIAM

I felt split in two. The pack was coming. Their thoughts reached for me like snaking tendrils of hot tar. If they found me, their influence would stick to me, suffocating me, rendering me unable to move or fight back. It's what they wanted. It's how they functioned. Submit. Submit. Submit.

But, while one part of my brain felt crushed by the power of the Chief Pack, something else equally earth-shattering happened.

Molly.

Her life force tethered me to my own soul, my own will. Her intoxicating scent filled my lungs, making me feel as if I could take flight.

Freedom.

Molly was my salvation. God, how had I lived this long without knowing what I'd been missing?

Jagger never had any choice. I understood it now. Though he tortured himself with guilt over the danger his decision put us in, he couldn't have turned away from Keara. I could never turn away from Molly.

She was mine. Her heart was my heart. It was more than just the connection I felt. I breathed when she breathed. It was as if every cell in my body had woken to her presence. How I'd lived without it I'll never know. She gave me the strength to push away from the Chief Pack even as they drew ever closer.

Turn away!

The pack's thoughts slammed into my brain. They were close enough to sense my mood. Their howls rose again as I ran toward the west. Ahead of me was the vast expanse of Mammoth Forest. If I didn't get more distance between us, they might be able to track me to the secret cave entrance. I couldn't risk drawing them there.

As much as it tore at my heart to do it, I turned south. I could still hit the edge of the forest and look for cover, but it was too dangerous to go to the caves. It was too dangerous to stay above ground. I had one advantage. Speed. The pack moved as a unit. I could zig zag and hope to throw them off my trail.

With no conscious idea where I was headed, I kept the tree line in the distance. Staying to the shadows, I prayed no humans would register my movement. To them, I was hopefully nothing more than a blur of motion. Something they might see in their periphery, but once they turned to look, I would already be gone.

It would be so much easier to shift again and let the wolf free. I could move twice as fast on four legs. But even that was too dangerous. My best chance of closing my mind off to the pack was if I stayed human. My wolf might become overwhelmed by the pack's pull.

With each step I took, my heart began to ease. As I moved away from the more populated parts of Shadow Springs, they grew confused. There were too many paths to choose from. The further they were from the Chief Alpha or whichever of his top generals directed them, the weaker the control would be. They would second guess and become disoriented. In a panic, they would change directions and try to get closer to him. I was banking on it.

They made one last rally, almost closing the distance between us. I ran along the rural highway. Up ahead, I spied a small reservoir beneath an overpass. I dove for it. Submerging in the cool water, I felt the last vaporous thoughts of the Chief Pack fade. They were still coming, but they would soon head in the wrong directions. I'd broken their hold.

Panting, I emerged from the water. I'd stayed closer to the forest than I realized. Water sluiced off my naked body as I scrambled up the hillside. Though the Chief Pack had finally given up the chase, they weren't far enough behind me to make me feel safe. Plus, I'd have to double back at some point to get to the cave entrance. It would put me directly in their path again. I'd likely have to wait until morning to even try.

It had been far too close a call. There could be no doubt the Pack had scented me this time. They knew I was close. That little piece of intel would drive the Alpha crazy. He'd likely double the patrols through Shadow Springs.

"Dammit," I muttered under my breath. Just up ahead, I saw lights. There was a neighborhood or campground about a quarter mile up the trail. My best bet would be to hide there for the night. With humans all around, the Chief Pack would have a harder time tracking me. Plus, I'd need to find a change of clothes. Mine were shredded in the alley by the vet clinic after my sudden shift.

Just thinking about those few moments with Molly nearly made my wolf tear out of me again. God, that would be a disaster. The Pack was way too close. They'd sense me in a second. I clenched my fists to my sides and tried to still my breathing. Molly might feel like my salvation, but she could also be my downfall if I wasn't careful.

The lights grew closer and I realized what they were. This was a trailer park. Soft laughter and the sound of glasses clinking rose. Probably a backyard barbeque or something like it. I stumbled on one great stroke of luck. One of the trailers on the outside of the park had a clothesline hung. Three pairs of blue jeans flapped in the breeze.

Darting quickly by, I grabbed one pair and dove back into the shadows. The fit was close enough. I stabbed my legs through them and zipped the fly. Now, I just had to find a hill to hide behind and bed down for the night.

The wolves howled behind me, registering the frustration of their failure. They would stay close, so I would have to stay hidden. I just prayed they wouldn't be able to scent my trail through Mammoth Forest from earlier this morning.

A car screeched to a halt just up ahead. My heart began to race anew. Shaking my head, I staggered sideways. No.

Stupid. I'd been so stupid. I'd run south thinking I could throw off the Chief Pack and keep them from finding the cave entrance. Instead, I'd acted on instinct. If I needed any more proof of what she was to me, this was it. Instinct had led me straight to Molly's doorstep. I may have protected Jagger and the others down in the caves, but I may just have led the Chief Pack to Molly instead.

I stayed in the shadows of three tall pines edging her property. Molly put her car in park. I saw her in profile. She gripped her steering wheel, pressing her forehead to it. My heart shattered. For as much as my own world had shifted on its axis, so had hers.

I owed her so much more. It wasn't supposed to be like this. When a wolf shifter found his fated mate, there should be heat, joy, and passion. I'd had no choice but to run at the moment her heart began to beat alongside mine. It wasn't fair. I couldn't protect her. Not like this.

She stepped out of her little red Honda. My wolf stirred and the jeans I'd stolen grew tight. She was only a few yards away from me, but it felt like miles. I wanted nothing more than to take her in my arms and comfort her. Let my heart warm hers and kiss away her fears. Because, she was afraid.

I couldn't read her thoughts like Jagger could read Keara's. But, they were formally mated and he'd claimed her with his mark. It allowed him to communicate with her on a nonverbal frequency reserved for true pack Alphas. Though each time he did it, it put Keara at risk. If they were close enough, the Chief Pack would be able to sense that, reading it as a violation. Again, I found a kinship to Jagger that now went deeper than blood. What it must be like for him day in and day out worrying for Keara? There had been times I and the others questioned whether the risk had been worth it. Now, with each breath Molly took, I knew it was.

She sensed something. I moved further into the shadows and tried to steady my pulse. Molly had her keys out. Her hair had come loose from her ponytail and fell around her shoulders in soft, brunette waves.

She turned toward the tree line. Pressing her back against the screen door, she squinted and looked in my direction. I held my breath. I should go. I should run in the other direction even if it stirred the Chief Pack scouts who waited for me there. Fresh terror poured through me as I realized what I was already willing to do. If given the choice, would I jeopardize Mac, Gunnar, Payne, Jagger, and Keara to save Molly? I couldn't let the thought fully form in my head. I wasn't ready to deal with the consequences.

I sucked in a great breath of air and made my decision. If I went forward, I'd walk straight into Molly's line of sight. If I went backward, that would put me in the path of the Chief Pack. My only option was to try and seek cover somewhere in the forest. I would have to run all night long.

It would have been a great idea except for one thing. I'd underestimated Molly's new senses. She took a strident step off her porch.

Then another. Squaring her shoulders, she faced the pine trees where I'd sought cover and headed straight for me.

"It's no good," she said, her voice catching. My blood caught fire as she approached. My cock stirred and I gripped the tree bark to steady myself. I could easily turn and vanish into the woods. She would never be fast enough to catch me.

God help me. God help us both. I stayed put and let her see me.

"Liam?" Even though she'd sensed me all along, Molly's eyes widened with shock as I stepped out of the shadows.

"I shouldn't have come," I said. It felt woefully inadequate. This woman deserved so much more from me.

She raised a skeptical brow and put her hands on her hips. "That seems pretty much beside the point, Liam. Can we talk, or are you going to turn into the big bad wolf again?"

A beat passed. Then another. Then, a hearty laugh erupted from my throat. God, she was right. So much of this was just completely beside the point. I got ahold of myself and grew serious. Molly's lips parted as she sucked in a breath. Being this close to me was having a similar effect on her as it was me.

"I meant what I said before. I'm never going to hurt you. But yes, I think we need to talk."

Molly cast a nervous glance over her shoulder. There was no way she could sense the other wolves like I could, but being around me had her on high alert.

"You might as well come inside," she said. Again, I felt split in two. I wanted nothing more than to be close to this woman. And yet, *being* close to her could make her a target if the Chief Pack tracked me to her. If they ever caught wind of what she meant to me… No. I couldn't even let my mind go there.

"I might as well," I said, trying to give her an easy smile. The truth was, Molly's trailer was probably the safest place for me right now. If I stayed among non-shifters it would be that much harder for the Pack to pick up on my presence.

"Good," she said. "I for one need a drink. You look like you could use a beer yourself."

She turned and walked back up her little stone porch and into the trailer. She held the screen door open for me. I hesitated, knowing once I crossed that threshold, I could never go back. I took a steeling breath and followed her inside.

Molly's trailer was sparse and neat. Everything inside of it was decorated in green and gold hues. She gestured toward her small breakfast nook, inviting me to sit down. I was so keyed up I wanted to stand. Hell, I would have rather paced, but I knew that wouldn't help ease Molly's nerves. So, I sat.

She was remarkably calm considering what she'd seen and been through. I could see her wheels spinning though. She sat, then got up, then sat again. I leaned against the soft cushion of the bench and watched her. A tiny bead of sweat dotted her upper lip. I had the urge to reach for her and brush it away. Her skin would sizzle beneath mine. I knew I could make the rest of her ignite as well. The thrumming heat between us was almost too much to bear. I half expected her trailer walls to blast apart from the combustible energy inside of it.

"You're a werewolf," she said. Not shocked. Not terrified. She had already accepted it. I knew it was because her nature called to mine. But, Molly was in no way ready for the greater truth. Hell, neither was I.

"I'm a shifter," I answered.

"And there are more of you. I heard them. You were afraid of them. Someone's coming after you. I could feel it. Why can I feel it?"

God she was beautiful. Glorious. She had the kind of beauty others might not see at first. Molly carried a hard expression, her face in an almost permanent scowl. A little line creased her forehead as she stared at me with those luminous sable eyes. Her thick brows cut in a straight slash above them, adding to the seriousness of her features. She had high cheekbones and a round face. Her full lips turned down in a pout I very much wanted to kiss away.

Her fierce gaze demanded an answer I couldn't give. How could I tell her what she was? What we were? Maybe I was wrong. Maybe I'd been so long detached from any sort of normal pack life that I wasn't accurately reading any of it. Even as I thought it, I knew it wasn't true though.

Molly was mine. She was my fated mate. I'd known it the instant I saw her. Had I any doubt, all it would take was the lightest touch of her skin against mine. My inner wolf clamored inside me, demanding his own answer.

I quickly learned Molly was the kind of woman who talked through her fears. Her voice raised half an octave as she got up and started to pace. "Liam, there's something. You did something to me. I can hear you...uh...I mean...I can feel you inside of me."

Her cheeks flamed red as she realized what she'd said. My aching need to *be* inside of her nearly drove me to my knees right there in front of her. Instead, I gripped the edges of the table and concentrated on taking slow, steady breaths.

"It's not really fair that you had to find out about all of this like that. That's my fault. I probably should have stayed away the minute I realized what you…"

"You *did* break into the clinic the other night though. Right? You took meds. Why? Did you think we would have some kind of treatment for what you...how you…"

"I'm not sick." My words tore out of me, taking on a hostile tone I hadn't intended. They came out in a half-growl that made Molly jerk backward. "I'm not sick," I said again, tempering my tone. "There's nothing wrong with me. What I am is natural. It's not an affliction any more than being fully human is for you."

"Then what? What did you need the meds for? I mean...we have narcotics locked up back there. You took Tramadol. We have stronger stuff. Morphine, even. You didn't take any of that. You took antibiotics."

I let out a great sigh. This was hopeless. How in the world could I tell her anything? We were connected, but she was still a stranger. I couldn't betray the others.

"They were for a friend," I said, knowing how weak an answer that was. "And I am sorry. I've put you in the middle of something that's got nothing to do with you."

She stopped pacing. Turning to face me, she took two steps forward then sank slowly into the seat opposite me. I'd been afraid to touch her again. Molly wasn't. She reached for me, gathering my hand in hers. The jolt of her touch nearly brought my wolf out again. My vision wavered and I knew she could see my wolf eyes glinting gold. Instead of showing fear though, my Molly marveled at them. She reached for my face and ran her thumb along my cheekbone.

"You've been here all the time, haven't you?" she asked, her voice a solemn whisper. "All around me. I don't even know how to describe it. But, I think I've seen shifters like you my whole life. I just didn't open my mind to it."

Smiling, I brought my hand up and covered hers with it. She was sweet and soft and trusting. The hint of tears made her eyes glisten, but she wasn't sad. Molly was humbled. It would be so easy just to sink into the feel of her. God, I wished things were different. Jagger had known. He'd tried to explain.

"I have to go," I said.

Molly jerked her hand away and stiffened. "You just got here. I have like a thousand questions."

"I know. But, I have to get back."

"It's because of those other wolves, isn't it?"

I swallowed hard and slowly rose. "Yes. It's because of those other wolves."

"Are you a good wolf or a bad wolf, Liam McConnell?"

The question took me by surprise. I had no ready answer. Molly didn't press for one. Instead, she rose to her feet and came to me again. Touching my face, she studied it.

"They've been looking for you for a while," she said. It was my turn to jerk away from her touch.

"What do you know about it?"

Molly bit her lip and moved toward the kitchen window. "Last night and the one before that. They were out there. I heard them howling. It felt like...I don't know. They were hunting for something. I went outside. Liam, it was the most eerie thing I'd ever heard. At the time I thought I was just imagining things, but now?"

I went stone still, afraid to breathe. I didn't want to transmit my fear to her. Molly moved to the back door.

"Don't!" I shouted out a warning, but Molly had already opened the door and stepped outside.

I felt the vibration low in my core. My wolf tore at me. My vision tunneled. I saw Molly in infrared and profile. I hadn't marked her. I hadn't claimed her. But, already, just being near me had changed her on a molecular level. She sensed the same danger that I did.

"Liam?" She turned to me.

A lethal wind kicked up behind her, tossing her hair straight up. The walls of her trailer rocked.

"Get. Inside." How I found the strength to form words when the wolf raged so fiercely, I do not know.

Molly took a step back, not quite able to separate the fear she felt pouring off of me from the danger behind her.

I went to her. Molly was already outside of the trailer. She gathered her arms around her, hugging herself as her hair blew wild around her face. I felt it as her spine turned to ice. The Chief Pack howled.

"Molly!" I shouted. "Get inside."

But, it was already too late. The Chief Pack had scented me. How could they not? As close as I was to Molly, I had to have laid a pheromone trail all along the edge of the woods. Stupid. So stupid.

"Come on!" I shouted over the screeching wind.

"Where?" Molly turned to me, eyes wide.

"It's not safe here for you. I can't let them figure out your connection to me."

"My what?" But there was no time for explanation. The Chief Pack was on the move. The pull to join them nearly drove me to my knees. Molly sensed it too. She took a halting step backward, her eyes lit with terror.

"Liam, you said…"

"No time!" I shouted. I had to get her to safety. There was only one place to go. I just prayed I'd be fast enough.

I went to her, gathering Molly into my arms. I held her so close I knocked the wind out of her. Then, I picked up speed and headed for the caves.

EIGHT

MOLLY

I couldn't breathe. I couldn't think. The ground whizzed by so fast it felt like Liam had taken flight. His heartbeat was my heartbeat and panic set in. The wolves moved in so fast from the east. There were three of them. I have no idea how I knew that, but I seemed to sense it through Liam.

All I could do was hold on tight as Liam ran on legs so fast they were a blur. I buried my face into his shoulder. His flesh seared me. His wolf hovered just below the surface. As he tore past trees and leaped over dead branches, I felt his bones bunch and roll. God, what was I supposed to do if he shifted mid-step?

I don't know what made me think to do it, but I repeated the same thought over and over in my head. "Stay with me. Stay with me. Don't shift. Stay Liam."

Impossibly, he responded. Just when fur began to sprout from his chest where I pressed my cheek to him, Liam took a great, steadying breath and I felt smooth skin against mine.

Then, we were alone. It was as if every woodland creature in a mile radius knew to stay the hell out of Liam's way. He stopped, finally. We were on the banks of a small spring deep in the heart of Mammoth Forest. I didn't know my way back. I thought he'd headed west, but the ground moved so fast, I couldn't be sure. The trees were so thick, I couldn't even see the stars to orient myself.

"I need you to trust me," Liam said, breathless.

I opened my mouth to say something, then clamped it shut. He regarded me with hard eyes. Then, he let out an exasperated sigh. "Fair enough," he said. "You don't have to trust me yet. But you do have to follow directions."

"I what?"

I didn't get a chance to say anything more. Liam came to me. He swept me off my feet and threw me over his shoulder. The ground came up with dizzying speed. He ducked low. Then, the ground opened up and swallowed us whole.

Liam stepped through a chasm in the rock I hadn't even seen. We came through the other side in pitch blackness. The scent of damp earth and wet rock filled my nostrils. Liam went down and down. I reached out with my hands, trying to find something solid. My fingers made contact with smooth stone.

"Don't struggle so much," he said. "We're on a narrow ledge and there's a forty foot drop on one side. You can't see as well as I can."

"There's a what?" I clawed Liam's back instead of the rock wall. He was the only thing solid to me. Without being able to see, I had no sense of up or down. Liam took two sharp turns then finally came to a stop.

He put me down but kept a hand on my shoulder to steady me.

"Liam?" I hated how desperate my voice sounded, but I couldn't get my bearings in the dark. My luck, I'd take one wrong step and fall to my death.

He scratched at something beside us. Then, light blazed all around as Liam switched on an LED lamp. It cast ghoulish shadows on the gray rock walls. We were in a wide cavern. Stalactites hung above us. We stood on a narrow path carved into the rock leading even further down.

"Where is this?" I said.

"Mammoth Caves," he answered. It seemed to cost him something to say it. He'd asked me to trust him, but I became keenly aware that bringing here meant he had to trust me.

"At least, that's where we would be if you headed about twenty miles that way." He pointed to his right.

"I don't understand," I said. Except I did. Strange as it seemed, the environment made perfect sense. That is, if you have some whack-ass preternatural connection to a wolf shifter. Which apparently, I did. I couldn't sense the other wolves anymore. This far underground with Lord knew how many tons of rock between us, they couldn't pick up Liam's scent.

"We're safe here," I said, my fear turned to wonder. I stretched out my fingers and ran them along the smooth, cool, rock walls.

Liam's mouth formed a grim line as he watched me. "To a point. Yes."

"How did you find this place?"

He shrugged. "Come on. I'm sorry it had to happen like this, but we need to go talk to the others."

"The what now?"

"The others," he said. "It'll be all right. I can't really hide you from them now."

My heart tripped. Hide me from them? I thought we'd just spent the last twenty minutes running from them.

With no other choice, I followed Liam. Tiny tendrils of fear crawled up my back as I realized I might not be able to make my way out of here on my own. Though Liam hadn't yet given me any reason to think he planned on holding me against my will, the realization that I was utterly dependent on him at the moment unsettled me.

A winding path had been cut through the rock. It was crude, jagged. Not like the smooth shelves in the Mammoth Caves I'd visited as a kid. I remembered at the time hearing the cave system stretched more than four hundred explored miles. The theory was hundreds more remained unexplored. I realized I was probably walking through passageways only a handful of people in the world had ever set foot in.

Voices raised in alarm ahead of us. Liam's back straightened. His thunderous heartbeat quickened. I pressed my hands to my ears trying to drive it out. I felt split in half around him. Whatever supernatural connection I had to him compelled me and made me feel safe. At the same time, it was foreign, mysterious. I felt part of something bigger and deadlier. I wasn't sure I was ready for it.

"Liam!" A deep voice called for him. Liam froze. He stopped so quickly I ended up plowing into his back. He reached back and caught me before I stumbled.

"Please don't tell me to wait here," I said in a furious whisper. "It's dark and I don't know where I am."

Liam's eyes flashed with kindness. "Don't worry. Stick by me and you'll be fine."

He took my hand and we walked toward the source of shouting. The narrow passageway opened up into a great, round cavern. Of all the incredible things I'd witnessed today, this may have been the zenith.

In the center of the cavern, three large men stood with their backs to me. They were shirtless, with broad shoulders and rippled muscles just like Liam. I didn't need to see their faces to know they were like him in other ways as well. These were wolf shifters. I sensed them clearly. Liam's posture changed. He moved ahead of me, shielding me with his body. I got the sense he didn't even realize he was doing it.

As we drew closer, one of the men turned. He was bleeding badly from a ghastly wound across his chest. Three great slash marks cut deep through his flesh. The skin hung in ragged flaps as the blood poured down his abdomen.

I gasped and covered my mouth. The man caught my scent. His eyes flashed silver and he let out a warning growl that I felt first before it reached my ears.

The rest of the group turned. In addition to the three wolf shifters, there were two women and another man. Human. How I could sense that now, I couldn't articulate. Being around Liam had changed me in ways I couldn't fully understand yet. In the corner, shrouded in shadows, another figure lay on the ground. I couldn't see his face, but the groan he gave out tore through me. He was hurt, badly.

"What the hell happened?" Liam said. He kept a hand at the small of my back.

"Is this why you needed the medicine?" I asked. I suppose I should have stayed quiet, but I just couldn't help myself. The injured shifter, the one still on his feet, had to be in shock. There was no way he should be able to stay upright with the amount of blood he was losing. Why weren't the others trying to help him?

One of the other shifters, the biggest of the three came forward. He was as tall as Liam, probably six foot four. He had dark hair and pale blue eyes that almost looked white in the ghostly glow of the LED lights. Strings of them lined the cavern floor. The

woman beside him held a lantern in front of her as they came
to us.

Liam moved again, putting his body partway in front of mine. My
skin prickled at his touch. The woman stepped forward.

"Who's this now, Liam?" she asked, her voice not unkind. She had
short red hair in a serviceable bob. It framed her delicate face. She
regarded me with an arched brow above clear gray eyes.
Human eyes.

"Molly," Liam answered, clearing his throat. "This is Keara. And
this is Jagger."

Jagger gave me a lethal stare as he put a protective hand on
Keara's arm when she tried to step forward to shake my hand.
She shot him a quick glance. He let her go and she came to me.

Keara was tiny compared to these fearsome wolves. She was my
height but fine-boned with porcelain skin. She wore a heather
gray t-shirt, jeans, and work boots. More appropriate attire for
cave-dwelling than my tank top, cutoff shorts, and canvas sneakers. Something about Keara's expression told me she noticed the
very same thing. She gave me a warm smile that seemed to say
she had a plan to take care of it.

"Keara Wilkes," she offered. "I'm pleased to meet you, Molly."

"Molly Ravary," I answered, shaking Keara's firm hand. Her eyes
darted up to Liam's before she stepped back to Jagger's side. He
still hadn't made a move to greet me. The man towered over
Keara like a stone statue. Whatever was going on, Jagger wasn't
happy I was here. What the hell had Liam walked me into?

"They're hurt," I pointed to the injured wolf. "I'm not a doctor,
but I know basic wound care."

"You're from the clinic?" Jagger asked in an accusatory tone.

"Yes," I said. "I'm a vet tech." I don't know why this Jagger had my back up, but I emphasized the word "vet." For my trouble, he emitted a low, threatening growl that shot straight up my spine.

"Enough!" Liam got in Jagger's face. There was something nonverbal going on between the two of them. In profile, I could see Liam's wolf eyes flash bright. Jagger's eyes flicked to me. Keara came in the middle of them, placing a palm on each man's chest.

"Heel, boys," she said smiling. "We've got a lot of work to do tonight. Liam, as you can see, Mac ran into a little bit of trouble on his supply run."

Mac, I deduced, was the injured wolf. Sweat caked his brow, but he seemed impervious to the massive wound on his chest. I moved toward him on instinct. Didn't anyone else realize the man was in shock? At the least, he needed to be off his damn feet.

The shifter beside him raised a brow but made no move to stop me as I moved around Liam and approached Mac. "What did you do with the stuff you took from the clinic?" I turned back to Liam.

"What did I? What?"

The corner of Keara's mouth lifted in a smile as she crossed her arms and looked up at Liam. "I think I like her already, Liam."

"I don't," Jagger growled. "I mean, I'm sorry. Liam, you should have given us a warning."

Liam turned to him. "Wasn't time. Three pack members scented me near the clinic. Molly thinks the same ones were prowling around her place the night before."

The amusement dropped from Keara's eyes. She put a hand over her mouth. Her alarm transmitted to me, and I straightened my back.

"It's all right," Liam said. "They didn't pick up her trail. They're not after you, Molly. They're after us. You're safe here for now."

"That's great," I said. "At some point, I'd really love it if one of you bothered to explain to me what the hell is going on."

"We don't have time for this, Liam!" Jagger turned on him, squaring off. This time, Keara didn't get in the middle of them. Instead, she came to me.

"Listen," she said. "These boys have some stuff to sort out. You'll have to excuse their lack of manners. Things being what they are, I'd say you're bunking with us tonight. At least until Liam can make sure the pack patrol has moved on."

"Pack patrol? I don't get any of this. I'm sorry. I'm hanging on by a very thin thread right now. And you've got a man bleeding out right in front of you and nobody seems to want to help him. And I can't even begin to assess the other one in the corner."

Mac started to laugh. "What, this?" He pointed to the garish wound on his chest. Now that I was close enough to really see it, there was no mistaking what it was. The three jagged lines ripped through his flesh were clearly claw marks. The only type of creature I'd seen big and deadly enough to make that kind of wound was currently standing all around me.

"It's just a scratch, darlin'," Mac said. "Ran into a scrapper. Just a low-level minion. He didn't know shit. And this? It'll heal up by morning." To prove his point, Mac thumped his chest just above the wound. He didn't even flinch. My attention was drawn to the space above his fist. On his upper chest, Mac had an identical tattoo to Liam's. A howling wolf's head framed by massive wings and crossed swords. I looked closer, Mac shared other features with Liam besides the ink. He had the same shade of ginger hair that looked brown in the shadows. They were similar enough to be brothers.

"He's right," Keara said, putting a hand on my back. "Shifters heal fast. If he's lucky, Mac won't even scar."

"Then why do you all have Liam out there committing about three different felonies and stealing vet meds if not for this?"

"I told you, we don't have *time* for this!" Jagger practically barked his words. Liam growled beside him. The tension between them stirred up Mac and the other shifter beside him.

"Listen," Keara said. "Mac, Gunnar, why don't you go someplace quiet with Liam and Jagger. Sort your shit out. It'll give Molly and me a chance to get to know each other a little better. She's a guest here, after all. And she might be willing and able to help us if the four of you don't scare her off. You're doing a good job of it. Now, git. I'll find her someplace suitable to hunker down for the night."

Liam straight up snarled. The others joined Jagger's side. It may have been just a trick of the shadows, but Mac's chest wound wasn't bleeding anymore. He moved and walked as if it was nothing more than a hangnail.

"Molly should stay with me," Liam said.

"No." My answer ripped from my throat. Though the compulsion to be near Liam still burned strong within me, my curiosity burned even hotter. "I'll hang out with Keara, if you don't mind. Let me see if I can be of some help, at least."

Keara made a shooing gesture with her hands. For her trouble, Liam gave her a full-throated growl, but I could tell he was teasing her. Mac stepped around us, bringing Gunnar, the fourth shifter, along with him. Then, all four men left the room.

"Sorry about that," Keara said.

"Keara?" In all the commotion, I'd barely registered the two others hanging back in the shadows of the rotunda. A middle-aged man and woman stepped forward now. Their companion still lay prostrate on the ground. He'd stopped groaning. That wasn't at all a good sign. The older man wore a golf shirt over a pot belly and had just a few wisps left of silvery hair. His companion, a thin woman with darkly dyed hair and thick glasses, hung back a bit.

"Thanks, Bernie," Keara said. "You sure you guys are all right?"

Bernie smiled. "Thank God Mac was there. I swear those patrols looked out to kill tonight. I've never seen 'em get that close. I don't know how the hell he didn't succumb."

Keara pushed the hair from her face and cast a furtive glance toward me. I had the impression she didn't exactly want me to hear all of this. Politeness might dictate that I'd excuse myself, but that wasn't really an option.

"You heard him. Just a low-level minion. It wasn't Ten...er...it wasn't the Shadow Springs general or anything. As long as you're all right," Keara said. She put her arm around Bernie. This drew a reaction from the woman I assumed was Bernie's wife.

"We're okay," the woman said. "But you've got to do something for Brady." She sobbed the last word.

"Let me," I said. I pushed past Keara and the others heading for who I assumed was Brady on the ground. I had the presence of mind to grab one of Keara's lanterns.

When I got close enough, my heart dropped. Brady was just a kid. He'd looked so big. He was a shifter, to be sure, but he had the fresh, rosy, unshaven cheeks of a twelve or thirteen-year-old. I approached him slowly, like I do any wounded animal. I bent low and held my hand out. Using my best bedside manner, I smiled and held a hand out to him.

"Careful there," Bernie said, drawing close. "Brady's got a bite on 'im. He's a good boy."

"Is he yours?" I asked. The wet shine in Bernie's eyes gave me all the answer I needed.

"He's our grandson," he said. "He's all we got left."

"She doesn't need to know any of it," Brady said. He tried to make himself small, turning toward the wall. I could instantly see the problem. Brady had three red claw marks across his arm and his shoulder was popped out of its socket.

"I can help with that, I think," I said. The minute I did, I realized it would probably be easier if Brady were in his wolf form. I'd assisted on dislocations with a couple of German shepherds before.

"I can do it myself." Brady gave me a determined stare. Sweat poured from his brow and before I could stop him, he rolled over and jammed his shoulder against the wall. The sickening pop sent empathy pain shooting straight through me, and I cried out along with him. But, he'd done it. I didn't give Brady a choice. I gently took his arm and examined it. He indeed had done it himself.

"Let me at least wrap that for you so it doesn't move," I said. "And some of that Tramadol Liam took from the clinic wouldn't go to waste here. What do you weigh, Brady?"

Keara came to my side with one of the green pill bottles from the clinic. I counted out the pills and handed them to Brady. I got a fearsome pout for my trouble, but he took the pills.

I dusted off my legs and stood. If I expected gratitude from Brady's grandparents, I was soon disappointed.

"This can't go on, Keara," the older woman said. Her eyes darted from me to Keara.

"Ellie, don't start," Bernie cautioned her.

Ellie's face looked ashen. For a moment, I thought she might vomit. Instead, she started pacing at the other end of the round cavern. There were boxes stacked along the wall. A few scattered ones on the floor sat open. Inside, I could see canned goods, loaves of bread, and other groceries.

My wheels started to turn. With the medicine Liam had stolen from the clinic, it became abundantly clear that perhaps Liam and the others were planning on staying down in these caves for the long haul. But, if Mac or the other shifters didn't have to worry about getting injured the way Keara might, what in God's name did they need the drugs for? If Brady was a shifter like them, why wasn't he healing the way Mac seemed to be?

"I mean it," Ellie's voice rose and echoed across the open space. "I didn't sign up for this, Keara. Those wolves would have killed Brady. It wasn't just some warning. What do you think's gonna happen if one of 'em gets their claws into Bernie...or me? They're after Brady now, and you know it."

Keara let out a great sigh. "They won't. Now, it's been a long day, Ellie. I can never thank you enough for what you've done. I can handle the rest of this. You two can clear out if you want. You're also welcome to sleep here tonight if you'd rather. I think it's best if Brady stays underground for at least tonight."

"Nothing doing," Ellie said. She went to her husband and peeled him away from Keara's grip. She looked at me and pointed a crooked finger at my chest.

"Nothing but trouble, if you ask me," she said. "It's too late for Keara, but it probably isn't too late for you, honey."

"Ellie!" Bernie grabbed his wife by the arm and pulled her away. "You mind your own business, now. Thanks for the offer, sweetie, but I'd just as soon sleep in my own bed tonight."

"Is it safe?" Ellie asked, eyes wide. She went to her grandson on the ground. "Honey, I don't wanna leave you, but Keara's probably right about this one thing."

"I'm fine," Brady said, but he wouldn't look at her. He kept his gaze fixed on the wall.

"Of course it's safe," Keara said, letting her voice drop to a comforting level. "Mac and Gunnar wouldn't have left your side if it weren't. Do you want me to go find one of them to show you the way out, or are you comfortable on your own? Brady will be just fine down here. We'll let him get some rest and have him back in the store by morning."

"Oh, we're heading out of here alone," Ellie answered for Bernie. "Those two have brought us enough trouble. Come on." She jerked her arm away from her husband, picked up a flashlight off the ground, and trudged toward a darkened passageway on the other side of the cavern. I made a note of it. Ellie seemed confident in where she was going. Heaving a great sigh, Bernie put a hand on Keara's arm and shook his head.

"She'll calm down some," he said. "Don't worry." He went to his grandson and smoothed back his unruly brown hair. But, Brady wasn't ready to give his grandfather any more peace of mind than his grandmother.

Keara stepped between them and touched Bernie's cheek. "I know. And I'm sorry things got heavy. We'll skip your place for the next two weeks."

Bernie's face dropped. "Oh, honey. I didn't mean…"

"No, it's okay. We need to stagger the routine a bit anyway. And you've taken such good care of us, we pretty much have a surplus."

Bernie looked at the boxes and scratched his head. "Well, you're a lousy liar, honey. But, you sure are pretty when you do it. We'll see you in three weeks then. I'll make sure to set something special aside for you. You just take care of my most precious cargo down here and we're square, sugar."

Keara went up on her tiptoes and kissed Bernie. He blushed. It seemed Ellie had some sixth sense of her own. She took that exact moment to call after Bernie to tell him to get a move on. He chuckled and did a little two-step before heading up the same passageway after his wife.

This left Keara and me alone with Brady brooding in the corner. Her shoulders dropped as if now that Bernie and Ellie were gone, she could let go of whatever pretense she'd been holding. She turned to me and smiled.

"Well," she said. "Guess you could say you've jumped into this with both feet, huh?"

I flapped my arms in exasperation. "I don't even know what to say, Keara. Near as I can figure, I've stumbled into a group of werewolf preppers. What you're prepping for is what has me terrified."

Keara reared back a bit, absorbing my words. Then, she let out a genuine belly laugh. "Well, except for the werewolf part, you've just about got it figured. There's no such thing as werewolves, Molly. These boys are shifters."

Not wanting to debate semantics, I went over to the nearest box and flipped open the lid. Baked beans, canned meat, canned veggies. "Well," I said. "I suppose it should comfort me that these *boys* eat camp food instead of...well...me."

"Oh, they hunt," she said. "They're men. They prefer venison. I'm working out how to store that down here too. I need more generators. Actually, I'm hoping Bernie will hook me up with another contact."

"What are you hiding from?" I said, straightening. "And why the drug stockpile? If Mac can heal from a wound that grave overnight, it's not like you're going to need the painkillers and antibiotics Liam took."

I walked to the other side of the antechamber away from Brady. I lowered my voice but guessed it might not matter. If Brady was a shifter, he probably had ears at least as good as a cocker spaniel.

"What's wrong with him?"

Keara let out a sigh. "He's just young, that's all. Hasn't come into his full strength like the grown men have, yet. And he's being raised by two non-shifters that are getting on in years. It's frustrating for him not having a real father figure in his life. Fourteen is hard no matter what species you are."

Keara chewed the inside of her cheek. If I had to guess, she was gauging how much more to tell me.

"I didn't turn Liam in," I said. "I had the chance to. In fact, I lied for him. I still don't know why. But, geez, Keara. Even if I wanted to tell anyone about this place or those boys, who would believe me?"

Keara gave me a kind smile. "Oh, more people than you think. Shadow Springs has been overrun by shifters for two generations. Most folk just look the other way or explain it away. It's easier to deny what's right in front of you."

It seemed such an odd thing to say, except the instant she did, it felt right. I should have been shocked when Liam shifted in front of me. Instead, it felt...normal...somehow. Logical. Like finding out the truth about Santa and realizing it was the only thing that made sense.

"But what are you hiding from down here? The pack? Those wolves that chased us? Keara, what would have happened if they caught Liam?"

Keara's face darkened. "Maybe you've had enough truth for one day, Molly. Why don't we just get you set up for the night?"

"No. I want to know."

She took one great breath and let it out in a whoosh. "I think you already know. I think you sensed it. But Molly, if those wolves had gotten ahold of Liam tonight, they probably wouldn't have just let him die. They would have just made him want to."

NINE

LIAM

"You should have told us!" Jagger slammed his fist against the cave wall, causing rocks to rain down on all of our heads. The growl erupting from his chest moved through me, calling to my own wolf.

Mac and Gunnar hung back, letting Jagger do most of their venting for them. I held my ground. Leaning against the mouth of the small cavern, I waited for Jagger to finish. He'd been like this ever since we left Bernie, Brady, and the women in what we now called the Supply Cavern.

"Exactly what was I supposed to say?" I said. I projected calm, but inside I raged just as fiercely as Jagger did. "Keara made it pretty clear we needed a contact for medicine. Well, I found one."

Jagger whirled on me. His wolf eyes blazed. He knew better than to take another step toward me. In this close a space, one of us would get hurt if it came to blows.

"She's not just a contact," Jagger said. His pursed his lips together, trying...and failing...to hold back his temper.

"What would you have me do?" I asked. "Should I have just left her up there for the Chief Pack to find? What if they'd tracked me back to the clinic through her? Molly doesn't deserve to get hurt because of me."

Jagger let out a bitter laugh. Mac and Gunnar stayed strangely quiet. Of all of us, Jagger should have understood better than anyone why protecting Molly meant so much to me. He'd told all of us for the last year how it was when he saw her the first time. He'd known in an instant they were fated. It was no different between Molly and me. Except so far, I'd had the strength not to act on it. If I were a bigger man, maybe I wouldn't have chosen that moment to throw that in his face.

"Relax, Jagger," I said. "I'm strong enough not to do anything I can't take back."

He curled his fist and dug it into his thigh. Flaring his nostrils, he turned away from me, shoulders hunched. Jagger's need to shift to process his rage burned through him. He was my cousin, but not my Alpha. Still, the tension boiling off of him affected us all.

"Does she know?" Mac finally spoke up. The wound on his chest had all but healed. Dried blood covered him.

I couldn't bring myself to admit the truth to any of them yet, even though they were all shrewd enough to pick up on it. Molly was mine. They could sense it the same way we all felt Jagger's connection to Keara.

"About what?" I asked. "She knows the Chief Pack Patrol is dangerous and out for blood. She knows enough to be scared of them. That's a good thing. She knows we're down here now and there was no help for that. As far as the rest of it? No. I've said nothing."

"You don't have to say anything," Jagger said through gritted teeth. "She can feel it, Liam. We can all feel it. And I'm telling you, if you care what happens to her, send her home and don't ever look back."

"How can you say that?" I pushed off the wall. "You of all people." I had to tread carefully. Every man in this room was here, one way or the other, because of the choice Jagger made. When faced with his own fated mate, he chose to break away from the Chief Pack to be with her. He was my cousin, my kin. Mac and I came to the caves because of him. At least, that's what I'd told myself up until now. Gunnar, and Payne? We'd collected them along the way when staying with the pack would have meant certain death for each of them.

"Jagger," Gunnar stepped forward. "Liam's got a point. Look, I don't like this new development any more than you do. It puts us at risk. You know how much I love Keara. Any one of us would put her life before ours. But it also makes her that much more valuable to the Chief Pack. If this Molly chose to be with Liam...well...then we're twice as vulnerable."

"She won't choose it," I said, my voice tasting bitter in my throat. "Because I won't *give* her that choice. Not now. We're on the same page, Jagger. But, you know I can't walk away. And she *is* in a position to help us. Keara's right. If we're going to be down here long term, we have to be able to take care of the people who come to us for help. Some will be human. Some...will be like Brady. Other shifters might not be as strong as you're asking me to be. And, God forbid, maybe someday it'll be Keara who needs antibiotics or some other medication. Molly might be willing to help us. She hasn't shied away yet."

Jagger shook his head. "That's because she's drawn to you. I'm telling you, the longer you're around her, the harder it will be to resist. If she *is* what you think she is, there will come a point where neither of you will be able to stop yourself."

"Well, we're not at that point yet, are we? God. I can't think of three weeks or three months from now. It's all I can handle thinking of three *hours* from now."

"I hope you're right," Jagger said, straightening his back. The rage had left his face and he cracked what might even pass for a smile. "For her sake, I hope you're right. Because, we've had two close calls in one night, Liam. It sounds like both you and Mac barely got to the caves. And Payne…"

My heart jumped. Payne. In all the excitement, I hadn't even bothered to ask where he was. He'd gone on a run up north, helping another rogue shifter cross the border. He should have been back by now.

"Anyone heard from him?" I said, giving voice to what we all feared. If Payne had been caught…

"Liam?" Keara poked her head in, preventing me from taking my mind to the worst case scenario. "I'm sorry to interrupt, but I've held your new friend off as long as I could. She wants some answers and she wants them from you."

Jagger and the others exchanged grave looks. I squared my shoulders and turned to Keara. "I'll take care of it."

My pulse pounded as I took the winding passageways. Keara didn't have to tell me where I'd find Molly; my heart knew the way. The air went out of my lungs when I saw her. Keara had made a discreet exit, leaving the two of us alone.

Molly stood with her back to me. Keara had set her up in one of the smaller caves and brought lanterns in so she wouldn't have to wait in the dark. There was a small pallet in one corner where the rocks had formed a natural ledge. Molly would be safe here. She might grow cold, but I longed to keep her warm.

She brushed a lock of hair away from her face. Her breasts rose and fell with her steady breaths. It all happened in a fraction of a second before Molly became aware of me. I felt the heat flush through her as she turned to face me.

"Molly," I said, my voice cracking. God, I'd been away from her for no more than an hour. I craved her touch again. Jagger was right. The longer I spent in Molly's presence, the harder it would be to tear myself away. I would though. I would find a way. Keeping her safe was the only thing that mattered anymore.

"I'm sorry," I said. "I know this has been a lot for you to take in all at once."

She drew in her bottom lip, deepening the dimples in her cheeks. "You could say that. I suppose I should be curled up in a fetal position somewhere babbling. Maybe I still will. It's just...I don't know. It all feels…"

"Natural?"

She parted her lips with a smack. "Aw, hail no. Not natural. I don't know what the word is. I was going to say...er...real. It just feels real. And I think that's because of you."

My heart lurched. Of course I'd be fooling myself to think Molly hadn't sensed the connection between us. Only I knew what it meant, but I wasn't yet strong enough to tell her. I could tell myself it was to protect her. There was that. But, the truth of it was, I was too damn scared she'd turn away from me. So, I was selfish. Jagger was right. Probably the safest thing for Molly would be to leave and forget she ever met me. The thought of that sent fresh pain ripping through me.

"Keara tried to explain," she said. "Some of it she didn't really have to. Those wolves out there. They wanted to kill you. Why?"

I raised a brow. "Kill me? Only if I were very, very lucky."

"Don't make jokes, Liam. I need to know. And another group of them tried to rip your friend Mac apart. And then that boy and his grandparents. Why? What did you do to them?"

I let out a sigh. How could I explain it all so that she would under-stand? I started with the easiest. "Mac's not my friend. He's my brother. We have the same mother."

Molly raised her brows and shook her head as if the facts I'd told her swirled inside of it.

"Fine. Your brother. I kind of figured. But, the Chief Pack," she said. "That's what Keara called them. I mean...I'm not an idiot. I understand a little about regular wolf psychology. So you, Jagger, the others. You're not your own pack."

"No," I said. "We're just...well...thrown in this thing together. The Chief Pack controls all the wolves of Kentucky. The Alpha domi-nates them all. His control is...absolute."

"What do you mean? Like a dictator?"

I nodded. "It's total though. The Alpha can make members of the pack shift when he wants them to. He can make them do...well...whatever he wants."

"Sounds like a tyrant," she said. "Like the thought police?"

"No," I answered. I moved across the room and sat down on the rocky ledge. Molly came to me. She put her hands on her thighs and slowly sat beside me. It was hard to think straight having her so close to me. But, I needed to get through this.

"No," I continued. "He can't control our thoughts. That's the hell of it."

"So he can make you hunt for him, act for him, *kill* for him? Even if you don't want to?"

"Yes. He uses his soldiers to help keep all the shifters under his dominion in check. He's got lieutenants who keep *them* under control for him."

"Those wolves who chased us, those were some of his soldiers?" she asked.

"They were."

Molly combed her fingers through her hair. She leaned back against the wall and drew her legs up. She hugged her knees and rested her chin on them. "What happens if you try to resist?"

I closed my eyes. The echoes of remembered pain shuddered through me. "Most can't. Pain. Madness. Death if you're lucky. It's more than that though, Molly. The Alpha controls how we spend our days. We don't get to choose what we do for a living. We don't get to choose mates."

"How is that possible? I mean...there are more shifters. So, somebody's mating."

I moved away from her so I could turn to face her. "The Alpha sanctions all matches. We don't get to freely choose who we spend our lives with. In most cases, there are no marriages. There's just...sanctioned breeding. My mother? Her match with my father and then Mac's father was sanctioned. Commanded. He's tried to breed out other Alphas. He's tried to genetically engineer the pack to be naturally subservient to him."

"Wow." Molly blew out a breath. "It hasn't worked though, has it? I mean you...and Jagger at least. You're Alphas. I can, I don't know, *feel* it."

"Jagger is my cousin. Our fathers and Mac's were shifters the Alpha controlled. Jagger's mother and mine and Mac's mother were sisters. Human sisters. We were always rebellious, but it was nothing that either of us couldn't control. Then, Jagger met Keara."

Molly's eyes widened. "He fell in love with her."

God, it was so much more than that. Couldn't she feel it herself? I knew she could. But, Molly was still trying to hold on to some semblance of her life before she met me. I couldn't deny her that. I couldn't burden her with the hardest truths I had to tell.

"Yes," I said. "And she fell in love with him. But, it wasn't a sanctioned match. The Alpha had other plans for her. When Jagger found out, he helped her escape."

"Escape from where?" Molly's voice cracked with fear.

"I told you. The Alpha controls who his pack members mate with. Keara was selected for one of his top generals. Jagger couldn't stand for it. So, he got her away from him. I helped him. Eventually, we found this place. In time, we found others who were strong enough to break the Alpha's hold."

"Until when?" she said. Horror written plainly on her face, she reached for me. "Liam, I *felt* it. I don't know how or why, but I felt what it did to you."

Silence rose between us like a thick fog. She knew I was holding something back. Every instinct in me told me to just take her in my arms. My need for her burned bright within me. How I found the strength to shield that from her, I don't know. With each passing second, Jagger's words rang truer. The longer I spent with Molly, the harder it would be to pull away.

She trailed her fingers across my chest. "This ink," she said. "I saw it on Mac. Jagger too. What does it mean?"

I closed my hand over her fingers. I couldn't think straight if she touched me. "We may not be a pack, but we have a *pact*. This was one way we sealed it."

"A wolf with wings and crossed swords. You're resistance fighters."

"Something like that. It was something Jagger and I did to honor stories we'd heard about men who tried to go against the Alpha fifty years ago and lost. Then later, when Mac, Payne, and Gunnar joined us, the tattoo became a test of loyalty. A commitment to the cause."

"I see," she said, her brow furrowed.

"So, now maybe you understand why I had to steal from the clinic. I'm not proud of it. We live underground to stay free of the Chief Pack. The longer I'm up there, the easier it is for the Alpha's soldiers to zone in on us. We survive how we can."

"Until when?" she asked again. I didn't have a good answer for her.

I settled on a simple one, "I don't know." It was true enough. "We help others where we can. Payne, he's the only one of us you didn't meet tonight. He's off trying to help another shifter cross the border into Ohio. We have a growing network of regular people who've been willing to help us. It's more than I ever could have hoped for. You see, it's not just shifters that face the Alpha's tyranny."

A shudder went through Molly. "Like Keara," she said. "Why her? I mean, she's not like you."

It was so hard for me to answer. If I even let my mind go to the worst of the Alpha's transgressions, my wolf grew fierce with rage. Molly could feel that too, even if she didn't fully understand it.

"There aren't very many female wolf shifters left in the world. My kind was cursed generations ago. Most of us are no longer full-blooded shifters. We have human mothers and shifter fathers, like Jagger and Mac and me. The Alpha has sought female shifters for decades. In the meantime, certain human women are just more suited for mating with shifters than others. I can't explain why. It just is. Keara was one of them. Except, she belongs with Jagger. The Alpha was willing to force her to be with his general against her will. It happens all the time. It's one of the things we fight the hardest against. It's the other reason why Mac is here. He has another half-sibling. A sister. His father was deemed important enough to earn two different women to mate with. Mac's sister Lena is human though. She disappeared a few months ago. We think she's been taken by the Alpha to breed with another shifter."

A tear fell from Molly's eye. She put her fingers to her lips. "I can't hear any more. I don't even want to believe it. But, I do. I told you, I felt it. Is that...were those wolves after me for...that?"

I couldn't help it. My wolf shuddered to the surface. I gripped the stone bench and my vision wavered. I was in danger of shifting right there in front of her. In the end, it was Molly's calm touch against my thigh that helped me put the wolf under control.

"I won't let that happen," I said. "*We* won't let that happen."

"And what about Brady? There's something wrong with him. I could see it. He wouldn't let me near him to do a full examination even if I did have the equipment. But, he seems sick. From what I've seen of you and Mac, you're indestructible. Why isn't he?"

Liam's face grew dark. "I told you, the Alpha is also trying to control the pack genetics. He can't have strong Alphas that might challenge him. So, a lot of mating pairs he makes are to produce betas and omegas only. He needs them strong enough to work for him, but not so strong to rebel. There are a lot of boys like Brady in that generation. He's considered an undesirable, but it's the Alpha's own breeding policies that made him. It's sick."

"What's going to happen to him...if..." Molly covered her mouth with her hand, as if the rest of her sentence just hurt too much to say.

She saw the answer in my eyes. There was no good outcome for boys like Brady. If he couldn't do the physical work the Alpha needed, if he couldn't be a good soldier, he'd be shipped off and exterminated.

Molly sat back hard. "I want to help you."

My throat grew thick with emotion. "Molly."

"I mean it. I get it. You need meds. It's less dangerous for you to get them from the clinic then say a hospital or doctor's office. It's smart, really. But, you also know it's temporary. Someone's going to figure it out. I have some ideas though. I think I know a way to get you some antibiotics and other essential medical supplies for the short term."

"I can't ask that of you. It's too dangerous for you. I've taken enough. Your boss won't suspect you of anything the way things stand right now."

"Liam, you said yourself you're building a network of people to help you. I'm offering to be part of it. For a little while, at least. It's not your call, anyway. I've already told Keara I'm willing to help."

Her eyes widened as I let out a protective growl. God, if anything happened to her. No. I wouldn't let it. I'd die before any harm came to Molly.

"On one condition," she said, her voice low and solemn.

I wanted to tell her I'd do anything for her, but sensed it would spook her. "What is it?"

"I need you to let me go home. Now. Tonight."

The wolf thrashed inside of me. More than anything, I wanted to keep Molly close to keep her safe. I couldn't though, and we both knew it. The safest thing for Molly was to stay away from me.

"All right," I said, feeling like my own voice had betrayed me. Sending Molly away from me went against every instinct I had.

TEN

MOLLY

The next two weeks brought torture unlike I'd ever known. Liam blindfolded me and brought me out of the caves that morning. I told him I'd never be able to find my way back even without the blindfold, but he insisted it was for my own safety as well as the others hiding below. When we reached the edge of the woods near my trailer park, my heart ruptured when I turned to say goodbye.

It had been like that ever since. Without Liam nearby, it was as if the air had grown thicker. Each rising of the wind, every car horn, I found myself jumping out of my skin listening for a wolf's howl. It wasn't me I worried about. Now that I had a sense of the danger Liam and the others faced from the Chief Pack, I couldn't keep the nightmare scenarios out of my imagination. What if Liam were captured?

I busied myself at the clinic. Bess's disorganization worked to my advantage. How she'd avoided being audited by the FDA boggled my mind. Once I'd committed myself to the task, stockpiling medication for Keara was easy. I started small with antibiotics and non-narcotic pain medication. Then, I grew bolder. With no idea how long Keara and the others might need to stay in the caves, I started thinking about helping her set up a mini operating room. Of course, someday she'd need someone qualified to run it.

"Everything okay back here?" Bess poked her head in as I stacked rolls of gauze in one of the supply closets. Her soft voice had me jumping out of my skin. I gave her a smile and went back to work.

"Just dealing with the drudgery, boss," I said. "Same shit, different day."

"Okay for you then. I'm going to head out. Taking a half day."

I peered out from behind the cabinet. "You? Seriously? What gives? Hot date?"

The minute I said it, my heart dropped. We hadn't seen a trace of Zeke lately, but I had kind of hoped Bess would stay single for a good long while. I didn't think the Shadow Springs Vet Clinic could handle any more drama this month.

Bess's odd expression spoke volumes. She was about to lie to me. "Nothing exciting. I just needed some time to myself. I haven't even taken a vacation in over a year."

Nodding, I finished stacking gauze and carefully stood. I'd pocketed several vials of canine insulin. Who knew what kind of medical crises Keara's people might face?

She could help, I thought, looking more closely at Bess. It was one thing for Keara to administer pain meds and treat cuts and scrapes. But, if any of her people required more serious medical care, someone like Bess would be a godsend. I didn't dare break Liam's trust though. He made it very clear that the Chief Pack had spies everywhere, human and wolf.

"Good for you," I said. "Take tomorrow off too, if you can. We can keep things under control around here. You don't have any surgeries scheduled." The minute I said it, I realized how badly I wanted her to. An entire day with Bess gone would give me gobs of time to put some plans in place about our next pharmaceutical shipment.

Bess gave me a crooked smile. "No. A half day is all I need for now. I don't want to get too far behind." She delivered the end of her sentence in a kind of sing-song voice as she turned the corner.

Blowing a hair out of my face, I turned back to the medicine cabinet and started making plans.

If Bess had been hoping for a quiet day after her brief alone time, the next day didn't deliver. We had two urgent care admissions first thing in the morning. Pitbull vs. Doberman mix. The pit got the worst of it. Bess called Jason in to help her stitch up the poor thing's nose.

"Sorry," Jason said. "Don't mean to leave you alone with the tech calls. You sure you don't want me to reschedule?"

I shook my head. "I'm good. Go help her with the combatants. I've got things under control."

My heart dropped as I looked out in the waiting room and saw the patients Jason left me with. Keara stood with her back pressed against the wall. She held a thin leather leash in one hand and my eyes traveled to the end of it. At a side glance, Jason probably thought it was a large husky. It's what Keara had written on the intake sheet lying on the desk. I knew better.

Brady let out a keening wail as soon as Jason closed the door to the operating rooms and disappeared. I tried to swallow, but my throat had gone dry. Brady didn't look good. When Keara stepped forward, Brady's step faltered. He crossed one paw in front of the other then sidestepped. My heart raced. That kind of altered gait usually meant something neurological was wrong. Keara gave me a desperate look.

"Come on," I said, forcing a cheery tone. "Let's get you back in Exam One." I cast a nervous glance around the corner. Jason and Bess were already in surgery. Tina was back in the recovery room with the Doberman. We were light on volunteers today. I got Keara and Brady into the room quietly.

As soon as I shut the door, I dropped the chart and went to my knees. I gently smoothed my hands over Brady's snout and pulled his gaze up to mine. His eyes were cloudy, his pulse erratic.

"What happened to him?" I asked, peering up at Keara. She sank to the metal bench and buried her face in her hands.

"One of the Chief Pack members came into his grandfather's grocery store this morning. He was alone. But, he got a little rough with Bernie. Accused him of price gouging out at the gas pump. It was all posturing. Brady got a notice the other day that he's supposed to report."

"Report?" I asked, straightening. Brady let out a pitiful whine and rested his head on his front paws. He was panting more than I liked, but his lids drooped and he looked like he was about to fall asleep.

Keara sucked in a hard breath. "He's going to be fifteen soon," Keara explained. "All able-bodied male shifters have to report to the Chief Pack. He'll be asked to serve as a soldier."

I looked back at Brady. His focus drifted in and out. I couldn't tell if he was merely depressed or if there was something more serious going on medically.

"Wait here," I said. I gave Keara a friendly smile and headed back to the supply room. Jason and Bess were still in surgery so I was able to easily grab the box of medication I'd set aside for Keara.

When I came back in, Keara was on the floor next to Brady. She held his head between her palms. He was still emitting a high-pitched whine. This wolf was in real pain.

"What is it?" I said, setting the box of meds on the floor. I joined Keara and pulled the pen light out of my pocket. The orbs had a milky quality I didn't like. I felt along his chest, over his ribcage and further down, looking for enlarged glands or telltale signs of what might be wrong with him. Though I had become quickly aware that canine and shifter physiology bore little resemblance to each other, I went to my comfort zone.

"Come on back, Brady," Keara said in soothing tones. "You know Molly's here to help. You're safe."

Brady nuzzled Keara's arm. He took in a great breath of air that caved in his chest. On instinct, I scooted back to give him room. Brady whined and shuddered. His head swung from side to side. Finally though, his fur began to retract, replaced with smooth flesh. It might take forever for me to grow used to the popping, bone-breaking sound of a shift. Liam did it with ease, taking no more time than the span of a blink. Brady though, the shift seemed to cause him agony. When he completed it, he lay on his side in a fetal position. The bones of his spine jutted out at sharp angles. But, he managed to get himself to his feet.

I grabbed one of the paper mats we kept on the exam table and handed it to him so he could cover his privates. Brady looked too ill to muster embarrassment though. He leaned his head against Keara's shoulder. She made soft, cooing noises to comfort him. For as big as he was, at fourteen, Brady was really just a little boy.

I expected him to withdraw from my touch, but he didn't. Gone was the stubborn kid from the other night who'd jammed his own shoulder back into joint. I ran my fingers along that shoulder and checked his range of motion. What drew my attention, though, were the angry welts along his other side. He also had deep bruising on both thighs and up through his groin.

"What on earth happened to you? Who did this?"

"No one," Brady said, his voice a defensive snap. Keara gave him a look then slid out from under him.

"Is there somewhere we can talk in private?"

"Why bother?" Brady said, his voice cracking. "I know what I am, Keara. Molly had questions about the Chief Pack. Well, aren't I a living answer? Take a good look. I'm a freak. I'm what they made me."

"Brady!" Keara's voice lowered to a hushed whisper, but her anger rose. She turned to me.

"Come with me," I said. The exam room adjoined one of the labs. With Bess tied up in surgery for the better part of an hour, it would be quiet there. We left Brady sulking on the bench.

I shut the door behind me and rounded on Keara. She stood with her arms folded in front of her, her color nearly ashen.

"He's not like Liam and Jagger," I said, stating the obvious. "He's weak. Why?"

"He gets picked on," Keara said. "I guess you could call it a form of hazing, but the other shifters near his age constantly try to test Brady."

"Liam said he's been genetically engineered or altered somehow."

Keara nodded. "Something like that. The Alpha dictates who breeds with whom. It's not natural. There's a reason regular Alphas are drawn to the mates they're supposed to have. It's a biological imperative that the Chief Alpha is trying to subvert so he can stay in power. It serves him to keep the other shifters in his pack weaker. Unfortunately, in Brady's case, it's a line too far. Shifting is torture for him. The other pack members his age taunt him. They beat him to see how much he can take. And in a few weeks, he's supposed to report to the Chief Pack."

I felt like I had needles stabbing through my gut. "What happens to him when he does?"

Keara walked toward one of the counters. She absently fingered a microscope. "I don't know what happens there. They won't tell me. I just know Payne and Gunnar got the worst of whatever it was. They'd be the ones to ask, but they'd never share it with me. I just remember how it was when we found them. They were broken. At first they seemed stuck in their wolves. Liam and Jagger are so strong. They're all so strong. They're meant to be Alphas. It's why they pose such a threat to the Chief Pack."

"Brady won't survive it," I said, feeling sicker by the second. "He'll get weeded out. He'll die."

"That's my fear," Keara said. "And there are so many more like him. I've been trying to convince Bernie and Ellie to let me take him underground with us permanently."

"And it's the main reason you want my help," I said.

Keara gave me a weak smile and came to me. She put a sisterly hand on my shoulder. "Yes. Once Brady and others like him live with us down there full time, they're going to need care. I don't know if there's a cure or treatment, but I want to try."

A heavy silence grew between us. Who was this woman, I wondered? She was soft-spoken and slight. Yet, she had iron strength running through her. She'd been willing to throw over her whole life for Jagger and these wolves But, something she said burned through me.

"Alphas. All of...your wolves in the cave."

"Yes. You have to sense that yourself, don't you? With Liam, I mean?"

I swallowed hard. My vision blurred and tears threatened to form. Yes. I sensed it. I sensed everything about Liam when he was near.

When he wasn't, a hole seemed to form inside my chest. It was as if I lived underwater waiting to come up for air.

"You said shifters are drawn to the mates they're supposed to have?" My heart jackhammered inside of me.

I knew the pull she was talking about. I just couldn't bring myself to face it.

Keara's kind eyes gutted me. She looked at me as if she knew my deepest secrets. "Well, it's like that with Jagger and me," she answered.

"How did...how did you know?"

Keara's eyes took on a dreamy quality. She took two steps back and leaned against the wall. She really was tiny. Though I was only maybe an inch taller, Keara was fine-boned with small wrists and collarbones that jutted out against the vee of her t-shirt. She was the physical opposite of Jagger. He was dark, looming, broad. She was light, her strawberry-blonde hair falling in waving wisps around her face. Light and dark. Sunshine and moonlight. And yet, anyone could see their connection. When they were in a room together, each seemed to orbit the other, always finding small ways to touch each other.

"I was born for Jagger," she finally said. "It's the best I can come to explaining it."

"Did you know instantly?"

A hint of a blush rose high in her cheeks. "No. Actually, I didn't."

"Liam said you'd been...chosen for one of the Alpha's generals."

The dreamlike gaze left her face and Keara's eyes grew hard. She pushed herself off the wall. "I would have died before I let that happen. Many girls have. But, many haven't. Brady's mother was one. She mated with one of the Chief Alpha's right-hand men.

They weren't fated. It wasn't natural. She was marked against her will."

Marked against her will. Ice bled through me. Keara didn't have to tell me anymore for me to understand. Still, she turned her head slightly so the scar she bore shone clear beneath the fluorescent lighting. Kera had a crescent-shaped mark at the base of her neck. Jagger had bitten her there. Her fingers went reflexively to it.

"Did it hurt?" I grew bold. I reached for her. Keara stood very still and let me, sensing what I needed. I traced the outlines of her scar. It was very faint, but raised at the edges. Tiny goosebumps ran down her neck at my touch.

"No," she said, finally turning. "It didn't hurt. If you can imagine, the craving for it hurt worse than the act of it. It was like a release, if you want to know the truth. But, that's because Jagger is mine. We're supposed to be together. For Brady's mother, she was taken against her will. I can't even let myself think about the hell that would have put her in. She was a prisoner to her wolf, not a partner. It drove her mad. That's what happened to her. Did Liam tell you that? Brady's mother found a way to end her life. She was that brave."

"Brave? But look at Brady. He's suffering. Surely having his mother nearby could have lessened that."

Keara shrugged. "Maybe. But he also suffered from watching her having to submit to his father when it wasn't her nature."

"And that's why Bernie and Ellie do so much to help you and the others. It's their way of throwing a middle finger to the Chief Pack for what they did to their daughter?"

Keara raised a brow. "That's a colorful way of putting it, but yes. And also because they're hoping we can find a way to get Brady to safety."

"Liam said something about that. The first night I came to the caves, he said Payne was out helping some other shifters cross the border into Ohio. Why don't you all do that? Why stay behind?"

There was a scratching at the door as Brady grew restless. In another few minutes, Bess and the others might come in.

Keara took my hand again. "Jagger, Liam, Mac, Gunnar, Payne...you have to understand, you have to sense it. They are so much stronger than shifters like Brady. They were meant to lead their own packs as Alphas. Most of the rest of the Kentucky wolves are betas or omegas even. Easier to control. So yes, it makes them stronger. But it also puts them at the greatest risk. The Chief Pack can track and sense those boys unlike any others. They can't get out, Molly. The longer they spend above ground, the easier it is for the Chief Pack to find them. Even if they *did* get out, they'd have nowhere to go. No territory to claim. They'd be hunted for the rest of their lives. Packs from other territories would try to drive them back. So, they do what they can. They help others to escape. They watch and wait."

"Wait for what?"

A tear formed in the corner of Keara's eyes. "I don't know. The Chief Alpha can't live forever. Rumor is he's in his eighties. That's an impossible age for an Alpha and he's... If it's true, no one knows how he does it. I think he draws strength from the wolves under his control."

"Have you ever seen him?"

A shadow passed over Keara. The question brought fresh terror into her eyes. It was all the answer I needed.

I went to her, putting a light hand on her shoulder. Keara had told me so much, but she kept some secrets to herself. "Did he...oh, Keara. The wolf you were meant for. Did he force himself on you?"

Sniffing, she ran a hand beneath her nose. "No. It didn't come to that. Thank God. And thank God Jagger never knew who he was. Even now, he'd try to kill him. It wouldn't matter to him that doing so would be so dangerous for all of us."

"That's your biggest fear, isn't it?"

She nodded. "That wolf is so strong, Molly. Not as strong as the Alpha, but I think he's strong enough to make any of our wolves submit to him. They can't get close to him. They *can't*. Not ever. And the Alpha, he can't live forever." This time, her voice dropped to a terrified whisper.

"Where is he? I mean...who is he?"

Keara brushed a hair from her eyes. "No one speaks his name. There are rumors, but the Pack keeps that secret to protect him."

"What are they afraid of? If he's so strong, what does it matter if anyone knows his identity?"

I didn't get a chance to hear her answer.

"Keara!" Brady shouted from the other side of the wall.

"He's got to shift," she said. "I've got to get him back to his grand-parents. The Pack's going to come looking for him."

"Come on," I said. "You can go out the back."

She put a hand on my arm. "Thank you. Molly...I know how much you've risked already. You barely know me."

I reared back. She was right, of course. But somehow, Keara was starting to feel like family. We walked into the exam room together. Brady had already shifted. His baleful eyes tore at me. As much as I felt for him, it strengthened my resolve. I picked up the box of medication and handed it to Keara. It felt woefully inadequate for what was to come.

"Next week," I said. "I'll try and get so much more."

Keara smiled and leaned in to hug me. "I'll have to send Liam," she said.

My heart tripped. I couldn't hide my gasp for air at the mention of him. So much of what Keara said drummed through me.

Fated mates. That's what she'd called Jagger. Her heart beat for him. God. Is that what Liam was to me?

"It'll be all right," Keara said, answering the question I hadn't voiced. She put a gentle hand on Brady and the two of them disappeared into the alley.

ELEVEN

LIAM

A month ago, I found solace underground. Now, it felt like the tomb it was. The tons of rock separating me from Molly weighed on my soul. Each night, I woke in a cold sweat, half man, half wolf, clawing at the stone walls until my fingers bled.

I told no one. Mac, Gunnar, and Payne knew something was off with me, but they didn't question it. We all had our own shit to deal with. Jagger was different. I caught him lurking near the tunnel closest to the alcove where I slept. His silvery wolf eyes flashed a warning.

I sat up, hiding my hands behind me. It was no use though. Jagger could smell the blood.

"You plan on doing something about that, or are you just going to drive yourself insane underground?"

I bristled. He'd caught me in the midst of a fever dream. Above me, the rock seemed to pulse. I knew in my heart it wasn't the rock itself though. Weeks ago, before I'd even laid eyes on Molly,

I'd found this cavern. It was a good distance away from the main passageways and antechambers we used. Something drew me to it. Now I knew. It was situated directly beneath the trailer park where Molly lived. Even before I laid eyes on her, her nature had called to mine.

"Why don't you worry about yourself?" I snapped my answer. The wolf was still mostly in control.

Jagger moved into the cavern. "I do worry about myself. I worry about you. I worry about Keara. I worry about all of it. She went to Molly yesterday. But, you knew that. You were up there too. Keara said you tried to be sneaky, but she can pick you out from a mile away almost as well as I can."

"You prefer Keara just waltzes through town unguarded? You were busy."

Jagger drew a hand across his face. He was hanging on by the same thin thread as the rest of us. I was being an asshole and I knew it. I also didn't care.

"It was stupid, Liam, and you know it. Keara's safer without us near her. And you know it fucking *kills* me that that's true. It tears my guts out. What the hell were you planning to do if the Chief Pack scented you?"

I punched my fist against the wall. The blood beneath my finger-nails heated like the rest of me. "You think I don't know how to stay clear of them by now? Jesus, Jagger. I've been doing it for more than a year. A hell of a lot more than you have."

"Maybe so, but you've been taking chances you shouldn't. Don't deny it."

I didn't. I sat as still as the stone encasing us. I couldn't meet Jagger's eyes. How could he of all people confront me on any of this? He'd taken his mate. In the two years since he'd found Keara, I'd never once begrudged him of it. That changed the instant I met Molly. Jealousy burned a path through my heart. I hated myself for it. But, I just...wanted.

"It's killing you," Jagger said. He took a softer tone and came further into the cavern. He sat beside me.

"I can handle it," I said through gritted teeth. "I've *been* handling it."

"I know. And I also know you're stronger than I was. By a lot. Don't think I haven't noticed."

A heavy silence hung between us. God, it hurt to blink. The bond Jagger and I shared had been among the strongest I'd ever shared with another person. Until Molly. Only I could never act on it without putting her life at risk.

"She's mine," I said, quietly. Admitting it to Jagger as much as myself. "I can't breathe when she's not near."

"I know." Jagger put a hand on my back. I flinched, but then exhaled, settling myself.

"She doesn't," I said.

Jagger let out a bitter laugh. "You really believe that? Come on, man. She knew you for, what, a day? You steal meds from her clinic and yet she turns around and trusts you with her life? She was all in the minute she saw you. She just didn't understand why."

I couldn't sit still. I rose and started to pace near the mouth of the cavern. God, if I could just go topside. If I could let my wolf out and run free through Mammoth Forest. I knew I could ease the ache burning through me. It wouldn't fix all of it. But maybe I could take the edge off the yearning I had for Molly. Maybe I could feel more like myself.

"So what the hell do I do with this?"

Jagger leaned back, resting one booted foot on the rocky ledge.

"Hell if I know. I think we've already established I'm the last person to ask. I did everything wrong as far as Keara was concerned. I should have been stronger and just got her the hell out of Kentucky. At least then she'd be safe."

"Is that what I should do? Should I ask Molly to run?"

Jagger shook his head. His eyes glistened in the dark. "I don't know. I know what I'd like to have you do. I'd like to have you forget about her and go back to the way things were. But, I know that's not an option. All I can do is beg you, man. For her sake and for yours. This isn't the life for her. Things being what they are, the best thing for Molly is to get gone."

I wanted to rip his throat out even though I knew he was right.

"I don't know if I can. Hell, you've met her. I don't know if she will."

Jagger stood up. "She's feisty. If it weren't for the fact her very existence could bring this whole thing crashing down...well...I think I'd love her a little bit too. Familial, obviously."

"You're a dick."

"Obviously."

The air changed in the passageway to the east. Gunnar came to the mouth of the cavern.

"Don't tell me you have bad news," Jagger said.

Gunnar grinned. "Is there ever any other kind these days? No, man. Nothing dire. It's just Keara's back. She said your girl Molly has another shipment. Keara says Liam should pick it up. She also said you'd know why."

Gunnar was also, apparently, a dick. He ran a hand through his light brown, surfer-style hair. I was beyond fucking with him though. All I could think about was seeing Molly again.

J agger was right. I hated him a little for it, but there it was. I stayed in the shadows as I always did. She'd put in a long day at the clinic. I watched Dr. Kennedy and four other techs leave the building. Each time the back door opened, my heart tripped a little even though I knew it wasn't Molly. She was deeper inside the building. Her sweet scent reached my pores and filled me with calming peace. Beneath that, desire simmered.

Finally, about twenty minutes after the last employee left the building, I heard Molly's slow footsteps on the tile floor as she approached the back door. She opened it slowly. Her pulse quickened. I let out a deep breath, slowing my own. In another instant, she'd feel the calm I projected. It was fake, of course. This close to he every nerve ending in my body felt raw, exposed. Animal lust coursed through me.

A sliver of light fell across the alley. I stayed tucked in the shadows, my back pressed against the brick wall.

"You might as well come in," Molly whispered. Her voice shot through me, quickening my pulse.

God, Jagger was right. This was dangerous. As Molly filled my senses, it got harder to listen for the sounds and smells of the Chief Pack. I moved quickly, joining Molly inside.

I towered over her. It took everything in me not to reach for her and pull her close. I wanted to run my hands along her bare shoulders. She wore a tank top again, her heavy breasts nearly spilling over the top. She covered them with scrubs when she was working, but now she'd cast them aside. Her own heat pricked.

"I thought you'd come yesterday," she said, her voice raw. She looked up at me, those luminous brown eyes blinking.

"It's better…safer…if Keara comes sometimes."

Molly nodded and closed the door. We stood frozen in the hallway for a moment. Both of us afraid to move, afraid of what might happen if her skin brushed mine. Except, I knew exactly what would happen. My body craved it. I curled my fists to my sides to keep her from seeing me tremble with the effort of staying away.

"How's Brady?" she asked. "When Keara brought him in he was...he wasn't well."

I didn't know how to answer her. Brady would probably never get better. At best, we'd bring him underground where he could live in hiding. His shift would always be agony. At worst, the Chief Pack would see how weak he was and exterminate him. He was on borrowed time. Both Bernie and Ellie knew it.

"I haven't seen him. He's probably spending most of his time with his grandparents now."

"But you have a plan for him, right?" Molly's eyes searched my face. She wanted pretty answers that I couldn't give. God, I hated this. I just wanted to hold her close. I wanted to feel the press of her breasts against me. My wolf stirred. I turned away so she wouldn't see my eyes.

"Liam," she said. It was my eyes she wanted most. Molly reached for me. Her fingers brushed against my jaw. An electric current shot through me. My vision tunneled and I could barely stay upright. My wolf's passion raged within me.

"Don't!" My voice ripped from me and I staggered away from her. Jagger had been right about all of it. Damn him. Just days ago, I'd been able to control this so much better.

"Don't," I said again, forcing myself calm. "It's better if you don't..."

"Don't what? Don't touch you?"

I pressed a palm flat against the wall, seeking the cool hardness. Anything to draw my mind away from the heat in front of me.

Molly came to me. She was bold. Curious. Fueled by a powerful passion she hadn't yet named. "I dreamed about you," she said. "It felt so real, Liam. It felt like you were in the room with me. But, I know that's not possible. I went outside. I was barefoot. I may be losing my mind, but you felt so close. What is this? You have to tell me. I have to know what I'm getting into."

I barked out a bitter laugh. How the hell could I answer that? What was she getting into? Just a thousand of years of instinct, nature, and magic. Again, I cursed Jagger for being so fucking right all the time.

"I think you already know." I hadn't meant to say it like that. I hadn't meant to say anything. I dug my fingers into the grout in the tile wall. Molly advanced.

"Liam...I want…"

She took yet another step toward me. Only a few inches separated us. My heartbeat became her heartbeat. My need, her need.

"Molly."

I should have been stronger. I knew what this was, or at least I should have. I should have listened to Jagger and never come at all. But, she was so close. She was mine. She was mine!

Molly went up on her tiptoes. Her hair fell away from her eyes. They darted over my face, searching for answers, searching for release. I wasn't strong enough. I ran my hands up over her bare arms, loving the way her skin turned to gooseflesh. Her breath caught and her breasts heaved.

There was a moment. A fraction of a second, really. Just a tiny separation between before and after. I kissed her. Desire poured through me. My wolf ignited. A lustful growl ripped from my throat as my tongue found hers.

God, she tasted so good. Thousands of years of instinct, nature, and magic. It all came spooling out of me. It drove the reason from my mind, the breath from my lungs. In its place was Molly. This was more than lust. More than everything.

She was mine.

Molly sank into the kiss. Her hands went up. Her fingertips trailed along my biceps then laced behind my head as she drew me even further down into her. I was unbearably hard. My fangs came out and the urge to bite her, to mark her raged through me. I knew she felt it too. I could sense it in the urgency of her kiss. All she'd have to do was turn, exposing the back of her neck. My eyes snapped open and that's exactly what she did.

Then, she gasped and drew away. The moment passed the instant she realized what it was.

"Liam," she said. She took two clumsy steps backward.

"It's okay," I said, amazed I could even form words.

"I'm scared." Her voice was so small. She shrank against the wall.

"It's okay," I said again. "So am I. I should go."

Swallowing hard, she nodded. "I'm sorry. I shouldn't have...tempted..."

There was a small cardboard box against the floor. Molly's eyes went to it. She pressed herself against the wall as I passed her. She knew as well as I did neither of us could resist it if we touched again.

TWELVE

MOLLY

Liam filled my thoughts. During the day, it felt as though I spent each minute holding my breath, waiting for the telltale signs that meant he was close. I would feel it in my pulse. Mine would grow stronger, filling my head until I realized it wasn't my heartbeat anymore at all. It was ours. Impossible as that may seem.

At night, Liam came to me in my dreams. I awoke aching for his touch, my sex throbbing as I chased a phantom orgasm. Everything Keara told me replayed in my mind. I wanted to deny it. It would be so much easier. But, the truth slammed into my heart with growing thunder.

I was meant for Liam. He was meant for me.

Fated mates. That's what Keara had called it. Just a few short months ago, I would have thought I was losing my mind. Now, it seemed I was about to lose my heart.

"You doing okay there, chief?" Jason leaned across the counter, putting his smiling face in my line of sight.

"What?" Absent-minded, I shuffled through some of Bess's notes. I'd gotten woefully behind transcribing yesterday's treatment plans.

"You've been off lately," he said. "Like you're in a fog. Something you wanna tell me about? Hell, you're starting to remind me of Dr. Bess."

"I'm what now?" I turned, facing Justin head on.

"The way she gets when a new man starts sniffing around her. In her case, we're always waiting for the next shoe to drop. You? Girl, you've been as dry as the desert."

I balled up a blank piece of paper and threw at him. "Never you mind. Pay attention to your own sex life. There's nothing to see here."

Jason snorted. "Yeah. That's my point. I've seen you though. You think you're being all sneaky. But, I caught you talking to that hunk of muscle out in the alley the other day. He's come around here more than once. You gotta introduce me to him."

My heart raced. I thought I'd been more careful. God. If Liam and I couldn't stay discreet around Jason, how the hell did I think we'd evade the Chief Pack?

"Like I said, pay attention to your own sex life."

Jason laughed and gave me playful but hard thump on the back. "You are so busted. So there *is* a sex life to pay attention to. Well, thank God. Michael and I were starting to get worried about you."

I was about to snap back a sassy retort when Bess came around the corner, her expression stern. She didn't like informal conversations up at the front desk, even when there were no patients in the lobby.

Jason cleared his throat and straightened. He shot me a conspiratorial wink then made himself scarce in the back room.

Bess didn't say anything at first. She hung back by the wall staring at me. I knew her well enough to guess what was coming next. She hated being a boss. Whenever she had to correct one of us or give instructions she knew we wouldn't like, she did this. She'd stare at us like a statue until she drew the courage to say her piece. Today, I just plain wasn't in the mood for it.

"Sorry," I said, turning to her and smiling. "Jason and I got a little bored. We'll make sure to keep the jokes to the breakroom or after hours. You should join us sometime."

Bess held a clipboard to her chest. She kept her weak smile plastered on then finally came toward me. "What? Oh. No. I mean, geez, Molly, I'm not that much of a stick in the mud. It's just, forgive me, but I overheard some of what Jason was asking you. Was he right? Is there a new someone special in your life?"

I took a beat. This wasn't the kind of thing I could answer yes or no to. Yes, Liam was someone special. But no, it wasn't what any of them thought. So, I gave her a non-answer.

"Listen, whenever I have something interesting to regale you all with about my personal life, I promise you'll be the first to know. What about you though? You seem...more content. Things all settled with Zeke?"

It was a little bit of a low blow on my part diverting attention back to Bess's wreck of a personal life, but it seemed fair play under the circumstances.

Bess's mouth formed a tight little "o" and she tried to figure out her own way to deflect. "Things are settled. Thanks for asking."

Touché, I thought. Bess Kennedy was the master of her own non-answers it seemed.

"Look," she said coming to stand beside me. She set her clipboard down and leaned against the counter, facing me. "We all spend a lot of time together in this office. I see you people more than I see my own family. And I know it's the same for you. I care about you, Molly. I like to consider you a friend. So, *as* your friend, maybe you'll take some well-intentioned advice. And I hope you don't think I'm stepping out of line."

My gut clenched. This wasn't like Bess at all. I couldn't imagine where the hell she was going with this.

"Go on?" I said, raising a curious brow. From the corner of my eye, I saw Jason poke his head out of Exam Room One. I tried to keep my posture neutral so Bess wouldn't look over her shoulder and see him eavesdropping.

"Zeke's got his problems. I'm not denying that. We're taking a break and he's promised to get some help. That doesn't mean we're ever going to be anything more than friends after this. I get it. But, he told me some things about some of the company you've been keeping."

My heart turned to stone. What in the hell was she talking about? What was *Zeke* talking about? I swallowed hard to try and keep my temper in check. Behind Bess's shoulder, Jason's eyes went wide as dinner plates.

"Bess," I said. "I'm sorry, but whatever you have to say, we're talking about Zeke here. To put it bluntly, I'd say he's a shitty judge of character."

Bess's face went white. She cleared her throat and picked up her clipboard, holding it in front of her like a shield. "I don't mean any harm, Molly. Honestly. But, if it's okay for you to worry about me, then you can't fault me for having the same concerns about you. I've seen you talking to that man from the alley a few times myself. Just be careful. I'm giving you the same advice you gave me."

"Thanks," I said, my tone clipped. I picked up my stack of papers and walked away from her. Fuming, I went to the back office to log in Bess's notes. I shut the door and turned on the television she kept back there. I cranked the volume up hoping it would give Bess the hint to stay the hell away from me for a few minutes if she walked by.

It worked for a little while. My blood pressure started to normalize. Then, something on the screen drew my eye. I hadn't paid attention to the channel; I just wanted the noise. The noon local news came on.

Still seething, my focus went absently from the images on the screen to the stack of papers in front of me, neither one making sense. How dare Bess try to lecture *me* on the company I kept? Had she not seen me take a damn baseball bat to her boyfriend to keep him from caving her face in? And it wasn't like that was the only time. Zeke was just the latest in a string of losers she hooked up with. God. It was infuriating.

Liam was nothing like Zeke. They weren't even the same literal species. I wasn't proud, but a part of me relished the memory of Zeke's face when Liam grabbed him by the arm that night. He could have torn him in half, and Zeke knew it. I saw it in his eyes.

I crashed my head to the desk. This was no good. Liam consumed my every waking thought, it seemed. On that score, Bess was right. I had to try and remind myself where I began and he ended.

Resting my chin on my forearm, I looked back up at the television. A perky, blonde reporter with big eyes and pink lipstick droned on as the camera angle panned out. Icy tendrils of fear crawled up my spine. It took a moment for my brain to process what I was seeing and hearing.

The reporter stood in front of a smoldering building, her expression grave. To her left, just inside the shot, a red Shadow Springs V.F.D. fire truck was parked at a severe angle against the curb. Water spewed from its hoses and firefighters emerged running. One of them shouted and waved to the cameraman and the reporter to step back.

My heart seemed to turn to ash right along with the flaming building. It was three blocks over. I shook my head, trying to deny the truth staring back at me in hi-def.

It was Bernie and Ellie's grocery store on Duncan Street.

My brain couldn't seem to hear or accept the words the reporter spoke. *Total devastation. Fire crews have been unable to extinguish.*

The office door cracked open and Jason stuck his head in. He read something in my eyes because he didn't say anything. He just edged his way in, crossed his arms in front of him, and watched along with me.

"Mother of Christ!" he said. "That's Bernie Langley's store. I do my grocery shopping there. He's got all the organic stuff Michael likes. Are they okay? Did they say?"

I was already up on my feet. "I can't. I mean...I have to go. Can you handle things for the rest of the day without me?"

Jason didn't take his eyes off the TV set. He just flapped a dismissive hand at me and crossed his arms again. "Go on. Get outta here."

My heartbeat raging, I edged around Jason. He slowly sank into the chair I'd just vacated. I grabbed my purse and ran down the hall. Bess called after me, but I couldn't stop.

Once the cool air hit my face, I caught a whiff of smoke and the wailing fire engines rose as another pumper truck whizzed past, headed in the same direction I was.

Bernie and Ellie. Oh, God. Brady!

I ran as fast as I could. My car would have been faster, but somehow, I needed to feel the ground beneath my feet. I broke into a cold sweat as I rounded the last corner and saw the inferno before me.

Giant tongues of flame licked the sky and a plume of black smoke rose high. A crowd had gathered on the opposite sidewalk, and I ducked a line of police tape to get closer. I had to see for myself. I had to know.

In the chaos, no one stopped me. Movement to my left drew my eye. Firemen in full gear stood around a large black canvas. As I drew closer, my insides turned hollow. It was a body bag and there was someone in it.

"Oh, God!" I covered my mouth with my hands and edged closer. Strong hands grabbed me by the shoulders and shoved me back.

Two firemen blocked my path. They stared down at me with grim faces.

"Ma'am," one of them said. "You need to stay back."

"The Langleys," I said, choking back tears. "Was anyone inside? Did you get them out?"

My spine pricked. A familiar sensation poured through me. In the chaos and tragedy, I almost didn't recognize it for what it was. Then, my heartbeat slowed and I locked eyes with the larger of the two firemen. He towered over me. His dark eyes flashed. It took only a fraction of a second, and a few months ago, I might never have caught it. But, I did.

I took a step backward, wanting to put as much distance between myself and these two as possible. They regarded me with renewed interest that made my throat run dry. I had to get the hell out of here fast.

"Are you a member of the family?" The taller of the two asked. I read the canvas strip at his right chest. *Tenley.* He came to me, stepping into my personal space. His brown eyes glinted gold. I might have convinced myself it was a mere trick of the light or a reflection from the flames. But, I knew better.

He was strong. God. Being near him seemed to ignite my nerve endings. It was so much like what Liam did to me except in reverse. Where my body seemed drawn to Liam's, this man's energy repelled me. Sweat trickled down my spine and every instinct in me told me to run. I held my ground though.

"No," I said. "A friend. I...I shop here. That's all. The Langleys are nice people."

"Why don't you come with us?" Tenley said. He looked at his partner, eyes glinting again. I knew with absolute certainty these two were communicating with each other on some telepathic level. Liam told me it was like that with pack members. I took a deep breath, trying desperately to stave off the rising panic. I stood no more than a foot away from two members of the Chief Pack and one of them had his hand on my arm.

"No," I said. "I have to go."

Shouts drew the firemen's attention away for a second. A beam cracked and part of the roof caved in on the Langleys' store. Before either of them could react, I was on the run again.

My heart thundered inside of me as I headed south. Instinct drove me. God, why hadn't I brought my car? The flesh burned at the base of my neck. It pulled me, forcing my legs to pump faster. I needed to get as much distance between myself and those men as I could. It would only take a split second for one of them to reach me. My only hope was that neither of them picked up on what I was.

Liam's. I was Liam's.

If they found me, if they caught me, they would know. I heard one of them call after me, warning me to stop.

Liam!

My thoughts, my heart called out to him.

A low, rumbling growl came at my back as Tenley broke away from his companion. I felt his footsteps falling heavy, vibrating off the pavement toward me. He knew. God. He knew. I must have been putting off some kind of wolf's mate pheromones and even in the chaos of the inferno, he knew.

I chanced a look over my shoulder as I came to the end of the street. Ahead of me, past the town square, the edge of Mammoth Forest loomed. Tenley had broken away from the rest of the firemen. His eyes glowed red as he watched me run. Even from here, I could feel his urge to shift rumble through him. He held his hands in tight fists at his sides, but they trembled the way Liam's did when his own wolf simmered.

Tenley snapped his jaw. Two other firefighters came to his sides, both of them shifters. They didn't give chase. Not yet. I realized with cold clarity that they were waiting for orders from their Alpha. It meant I had one chance to get the hell away from them before their decision became clear.

I turned and ran as fast as I could toward the woods. It was too late to head back to the clinic and my car. In any event, I didn't want to draw them there. Our work wasn't done. If the Chief Pack caught wind of the clinic's connection to Liam and the others, they might not survive the blow. The Langleys' store was already in ruins.

God. Bernie. Ellie. Brady. The image of that body bag burned through me. I kept on running.

My heart pounded so hard it felt as if it might burst from my chest. The pavement gave way to soft earth as I left the edge of town and headed for the dark expanse of the woods.

Liam. I had to get to Liam. I had to warn them about what happened. If I closed my eyes, I could sense Tenley and the others, watching, calculating their next move.

Bare branches clawed at my arms. I stumbled over loose rocks. I had no sense of which direction I ran. I just knew I had to keep on going. Maybe the woods would mask my scent. It was my only hope if the pack decided to give chase.

Gnarled birch trees and tall poplars loomed all around me. I tripped over an uneven patch of ground and landed hard on my palms. Blood welled there where I hit the jagged edge of a rock. I cried out but scrambled back to my feet. I had to keep going. I had to hide. Every instinct in me warned me what could happen if the Chief Pack figured out who I was. I was a wolf's mate. That's all they would care about. They would take me to the Alpha against my will like they'd tried to do with Keara.

I took three staggering steps forward. Rotted tree roots clawed at my legs, threatening to drive me back to the ground. I cried out, desperate to keep moving.

A howl rent the air to the east of me. My thunderous heartbeat took my breath away. But, it wasn't my heartbeat at all. It was his. I skidded to a stop and fell to my knees in the soft earth. When I lifted my head, I came face to face with Liam's wolf.

He blocked out the sun behind his shoulders, casting me in shadow. Liam's lips curled back, revealing long fangs. His ears pricked and his silvery fur shimmered.

We stayed frozen for a moment. Me on all fours in front of him. His hot breath blew through my hair. Liam stood tall, majestic. A soft growl rippled through him.

"Liam." My voice came out as a choked sob. I reached for him, sinking my fingers into the deep fur of his flank. His outer coat was rough, but beneath that, as my fingers touched his powerful thigh muscles, his fur became sable.

Liam lifted his head and let out a baleful howl that vibrated through me. Then, he dropped his head. His fur shimmered and his muscles rolled. The shift was effortless. One moment he was the wolf. The next, this beautiful man crouched before me. Every muscle chiseled to perfection. Liam's hair glistened with sweat.

My hand was still on his thigh. His massive cock hung before me. He was rock hard.

Gasping, I drew my hand away. Liam got his hands under my arms and helped me to my feet.

"What happened?" he said, his voice ragged. "You're hurt? I felt you. I came as fast as I could."

Shaking, I ran my fingers through my hair. I couldn't think straight. Liam's power drew me to him. My knees knocked together. Raw desire flooded my senses.

"No. It's not me. Oh, Liam. Oh, God."

He came to me. Liam slid his arms around my waist and pulled me close. He laced his fingers through my hair and caressed my cheek with his thumb. His skin left a heated trail over mine. My lips parted and wild heat pooled between my legs.

"Bernie," I gasped. "The Langleys' store. They've burned it to the ground."

I hadn't wanted to let my mind go there, but now I'd given voice to my fears. The moment I did, I knew the truth. "The Chief Pack. They were all over it. They're in the fire department. Someone died, Liam. They brought out a body bag. God. Maybe they all died. I don't know. But the store's gone. It's all gone."

Liam's eyes darted over my face. He wasn't even trying to hide the brilliant glow of his wolf within them.

I wanted him. Every cell in my body seemed to call out to his. Impossible. Maddening. I couldn't think. I couldn't breathe.

"Molly," Liam said, his voice choked. He stood before me naked. Beautiful. My own raw need reflected back to me in his golden eyes.

"You're all right?" he asked. His hands roamed along my jaw, down my shoulders, to the small of my back. "I thought...I felt...you were...terrified."

Nodding, I brought my hand up and put it over his where he touched my cheek. "They saw me. The Chief Pack saw me. I don't think they…"

"I don't care. It doesn't matter. You're here. You're with me." I think he meant it to comfort me, but as he uttered those words, I could see fresh pain etching lines in his face. Standing this close to me seemed to tear him apart in the same way it did me.

I couldn't take it another second. I went up on my tiptoes and found his lips. With my thumbs at his ears, I drew his head down. He sank into the kiss, groaning into my mouth. My nerve endings caught fire.

I was meant for this. So was he. There with the expanse of woods around us, it was as natural as breathing.

Liam tore himself away. His lips curled and his eyes blazed. I could see the beast within him, torturing Liam to get out. It wasn't fair of me. I knew it. Touching him like that, tempting him. It was selfish.

"I can't. Molly, I can't hold back."

I meant to tell him I understood. I meant to step away and remove the temptation of my body and my touch. But, the moment I tried, everything fell away.

"So don't," I said, breathless. Logic told me this was dangerous, but instinct drove me. Another wolf had gotten close enough to touch me. My body cried out for *this* wolf. It was as if I needed him to erase the threat of Tenley's touch.

One beat passed. Two. Liam's chest heaved as he made his choice. Then, he grabbed me, gently but forcefully. He threaded his fingers through my hair and crushed his lips to mine. The sheer force of it brought me down. We sank to the forest floor together until I was on my knees before him. Liam bent at the waist to keep his lips locked with mine.

He was so close. I reached for him without thinking. My fingers closed around his hardness. He jerked in my palm. Liam threw his head back and let out a plaintive howl that shuddered through me.

Before I knew what was happening, I tore at my scrub top. Casting it aside along with my tank top, Liam was already helping me out of my pants. He laid me down in the cool, velvety moss. He hovered over me for a moment, his tender eyes searching my face.

"Please," I begged.

It was so quick. With one powerful thrust, Liam parted my thighs and entered me, rooting himself deep. Still daylight, the stars came out anyway. I curved myself around him. I'd been starving for so long. As Liam began to move his hips, the world cracked open and my heart became his.

THIRTEEN

Liam

Molly. My Molly. I should have walked away. I should have heeded everything Jagger told me. But when Molly's lips brushed mine and I felt her heat, there was no going back.

"Please," she begged me again. She spread herself open. The soft, pink petals at the juncture of her thighs spread for me. She was wet, glistening, so ready. I picked up the faint scent of another wolf on her. It enraged me. She was mine. She had to be mine.

With my wolf spurring me on, I stroked myself and slid into her welcoming heat. Oh, God. She was heaven. I couldn't be gentle. Thousands of years of primal instinct took over and I thrust myself home. Molly's body curved to mine as she wrapped her legs around me. Her hard nipples brushed my bare chest, sending new waves of pleasure coursing through me.

"Molly." I whispered her name over and over as I fucked her deep. How could I have ever thought to deny myself this? I could no more stop myself from breathing. Neither could she. With each pounding thrust, she opened herself even more. Her sweet juices flowed, coating us both.

I wanted to turn her, take her on all fours and feed my animal lust. I knew it was too dangerous. The urge to sink my teeth into the soft flesh at the base of her neck burned too strong. And she'd let me. I could feel her own throbbing need for it even if she didn't understand what it meant yet. But, oh, God, how good it would feel. To mark her. Claim her. Make her mine forever.

"Liam," she cried, squirming beneath me. She craved my bite just as hard. I felt it pouring through her, making her whole body quiver. How I found the strength to hold that part back I'll never know.

This was enough for now. It would have to be. Molly started to come. I felt her hitch, trying to hold it back. I redoubled my efforts and drove my cock ever deeper. She clawed at the ground to get the friction she needed. I held myself still for a moment and let her fuck me back. One thrust. Two. Then her orgasm ripped through her. Her breasts shuddered. I leaned down and took one pink nipple in my mouth. God, she tasted so sweet. I wanted nothing more than to spread her legs and taste her sweet nectar as she coasted down.

But, my own pleasure crescendoed. The wolf took over. Digging my heels into the soft earth, I found purchase, driving my cock in as deep as it would go.

"Yes!" She cried. Oh, God, she wanted it. My nostrils flared as my breath came hard. Holding my weight on my elbows, I wanted to see her. I wanted Molly's eyes as my seed poured into her, heating her core. She tightened her legs around my waist, locking them at the ankles. It was the sweetest prison on earth.

A howl ripped from my throat as I poured into her even as I knew how dangerous this was. If any of the Chief Pack had followed her, they would track us easily, my scent hitting them like a thunderbolt.

But, the woods stayed quiet except for the sounds of our passion. Molly left a trail of soft kisses over my chest as I crested down and lay beside her.

We were awkward with each other for a moment. Though I hadn't marked her, we'd crossed a threshold neither of us could walk back. I didn't have the strength to say it to her then. I don't think she had the strength to hear it. For now, it was enough just to touch her.

"Liam," she said. "That was."

"Dangerous," I answered for her.

Molly gathered her clothes. I helped her find them and held her shirt out so she could slip it back on. It killed me to see her cover her body. I wanted to warm it with mine forever. Once she was dressed, she sat hugging her knees. My wolf stirred again. We weren't safe out here much longer. I could sense the Pack. They hadn't followed Molly. They were in town, probably drawn to the fire Molly told me about.

"Are we...I mean...I know..." she fumbled for the words. I crooked my finger beneath her chin and lifted her gaze to meet mine.

"We're like Jagger and Keara," she said. Such a simple sentence. The truth of it ripped through me. Of course I'd known since the minute I saw her.

There was so much more to tell her. I settled for a quiet, "Yes."

She rested her chin on her knees. "Okay."

I couldn't help it. Her straightforward acceptance of such an earth-shattering fact made me smile. It also shredded my guts.

"I have to get you home," I said. It hurt to swallow. My heart lodged in my throat at the thought of leaving Molly again. But, it was the safest, smartest thing to do. As long as she didn't bear my mark, she could still be safe in town.

"No," she gasped, the same hurt flooding through her. She pressed her palm to her ear. My pulse beat in time with hers now. It would grow stronger. If I ever did mark her, we would be connected on an even more powerful telepathic link. For now, her body and mine would be drawn to one another like a magnetic pull. I'd never feel whole unless she was near.

"It's safer for both of us," I said, hating myself for it. It wasn't fair to her. It wasn't supposed to be like this. Now that we'd coupled, I should have her by my side. I helped her to her feet.

We walked in silence for almost a mile. Molly's trailer park was just over the next ridge. Tonight, I would take little comfort from sleeping below her in the caves. She reached for me. I took her hand and kissed it. For now, this would have to be enough.

"What about Brady?" she said as soon as we saw the distant lights of the trailer park.

"I'll find out what I can. I fear the worst, though."

She stopped and turned to me. "Do you think the Pack found out that the Langleys were helping you?"

A knife twisted in my gut. I said a silent prayer that it was just some unlucky accident. I knew in my heart that wasn't likely. Molly knew it too.

"Molly," I said. "Until we know more…"

She took a deep breath. "Until you know more, it's better if you and the others stay away from the clinic. For a few days at least. I was thinking the same thing."

I pulled her to me, kissing the top of her head as she rested it against my chest. "God. I'm sorry. It's killing me not to be near you every second of every day. It's going to be worse now, not better."

A single tear fell down her cheek as she looked up at me. "Will you be careful? Will you promise me you won't do anything stupid or get caught? I mean it. I can bear to be away from you if I know you're safe."

Smiling, I smoothed the hair away from her face. "I was about to say the same thing to you. Don't do anything heroic. Lay low. Don't go to the Langleys' store. Don't ask around about them. I'll get word to you as soon as I can."

"They're everywhere, aren't they? The scene of that fire was crawling with them. It wasn't just the firefighters. God. How could I have lived in this town for so long and not sensed something different?"

"We're good at blending in when we need to," I said. "And most humans believe what *they* need to. They explain away unusual things as something normal. It's your nature. It's how you stay safe."

"So what do I do if I run into one of the Pack members?"

My heart lurched thinking about it. Every instinct in me wanted me to bring her with me to hide down in the caves. I knew it might come to that, but the simple truth was, she was safer away from me than with me. At least for now.

"Just try to act as natural as possible. I haven't marked you. They won't sense you."

She put a hand the back of her neck. Desire flared hot inside me. I knew it did for her too.

"You be careful too," she said.

I kissed her one last time. Through the brush, she'd find her way home. "I'll send word as soon as I can," I said. "It'll be all right."

Molly gave me a trusting nod and I prayed it really would be. I watched her straighten her back as she walked up to her trailer. She gave a bright smile and a wave to a group of her neighbors walking by. She was bold and fearless. My heart ached to leave her, but I had no choice.

The others were waiting for me as I made my way into the great antechamber. Only Keara was missing. Jagger gave me a hard stare. Mac, Gunnar, and Payne had the decency to look sheepish.

I couldn't lie. I couldn't hide it. I knew they could scent Molly all over me. We didn't have a pack link, but these men had spent enough time with me to know exactly what had happened.

"Are you out of your fucking mind?" Payne was the one to say it. That surprised me. His hair flamed even redder under the LED lights.

"What do you want me to say?" I said. The fight had gone out of me. Until Payne found his own mate, he'd never fully understand. I realized then that's exactly why Jagger kept quiet. He'd be a hypocrite otherwise.

"I haven't marked her. She's safe. *We're* safe. At least for now."

Jagger squeezed his eyes shut and pounded the back of his head against the cave wall. There was news. Bad.

"Where's Keara?" I asked, already knowing the answer.

"Bernie missed his drop," Mac answered. "Keara went looking for him. I assume you know what happened by now?"

"Molly said there was a fire. She said someone was killed."

Jagger's eyes snapped open. He ran a hand over his mouth. "She's back."

No sooner had he said it when Keara walked into the mouth of the cavern. The tracks of her tears lined her face.

"They're gone," she whispered. "Bernie, Ellie...and Brady. All three of them. Oh, God, Jagger." She went to him, crumpling in his arms.

FOURTEEN

MOLLY

Sex with Liam had changed me. He should have warned me. Now, it was more than just a familiar pulse I felt. Now, there seemed an invisible string binding me to him. It dawned on me the first night without him as I lay in bed in my trailer. Liam's cavern was directly below me. The realization came over me, sending pins and needles through my body. I threw off the covers and went outside. A light rain fell, making the ground soft and wet.

I stepped off my small, square, cement patio and knelt in the grass. Pressing my fingers into the earth, I felt heat rising up through the ground.

"Liam," I whispered. I felt his slow, rhythmic breathing. He was asleep. There might be miles of rock separating us, but he could have been standing right beside me. God, had he known? Of course he had. Why else would he have chosen that particular section among hundreds of miles of tunnels to sleep?

It comforted me enough to get through the next day. Still, I felt on edge, hoping to feel his presence. Hoping he would decide spending time apart wasn't necessary.

I busied myself with charts and patient intake. Bess had surgeries scheduled all day. She'd taken a group of interns with her, so it left Jason and me mostly alone. It's what I needed.

"How'd it go with your new man last night?" Jason asked, nudging me with his shoulder.

A felt my cheeks heat with a creeping blush. Dammit. My poker face sucked. "Never you mind," I said. There was no point in trying to deny anything. It would raise more suspicion than honesty.

"Well, good," he said. "Glad to hear one of us is getting laid."

I raised a brow. "Oh? Care to share?"

Jason shrugged. "No, Michael's just off at training for a couple of weeks."

I'd forgotten, Jason's partner served in the Kentucky Air National Guard. He'd been deployed a couple of years ago to the Persian Gulf. Jason had been a wreck the entire time.

I came up behind him and rested my chin on his shoulder. "Well, let's just say my new man and I are dealing with a forced separation of our own. Maybe you should come hang out with me tonight. We can watch '90s slasher movies and drink homemade wine. My neighbor makes it."

Jason touched his temple to my cheek. "That sounds like a slice of heaven, buttercup. Count me in."

The television we kept above the waiting room benches was tuned to the local news. My heart tripped as the scenes from last night's fire at Bernie's came on. Jason picked up the remote and upped the volume.

"This was something else," he said. "I walked by on my way home from work last night."

"What are they saying?" I asked, as ice filled my veins.

Jason stared at the screen, gesturing with the remote. "Arson, maybe. At least they're not ruling it out. One of Michael's friends from the gym is a volunteer fireman. I called him last night. It's awful. That husband and wife were sleeping when it happened. They didn't get out. You know that boy, their grandson?"

My throat grew thick. I gripped the edge of the counter, bracing myself for what I knew Jason was going to say next. Oh, God, I didn't want to hear it. "Brady," I whispered.

"Yeah. Sweet kid," Jason clucked his tongue. "He was up in the attic apartment, I guess. There's all kinds of rumors floating around. Like maybe the kid was trying to cook meth or something. I don't know. Anyway, he didn't make it out either."

"Brady's dead."

"Yep," Jason answered. "Breaks my heart. He was troubled, that kid. I thought maybe he was autistic or something. I don't know. Something. The Langleys were doing the best they could trying to raise him. I'd just hate it if they ended up getting burned alive for their trouble. Molly?"

Jason called after me, but I was already out the back door into the alley. I got as far as the dumpster before my stomach lurched and I threw up all over the pavement. Oh, God. Oh, Brady. There was no way this was an accident. This had to be the Chief Pack. They knew. They found out the Langleys were helping Liam and the others.

Clutching the brick wall, I straightened. If they could find out about the Langleys, it meant this clinic might be next. God, what would I do if anything happened to Jason or Bess or the others inside?

It meant we were out of time. I would have to pack up as many meds and supplies as I could today and get them to Keara. Then, we'd have to cool it until the Chief Pack moved on. I just prayed she'd have enough to last for a while.

I ignored Jason's questions when I went back inside. It was now or never. I made some excuse about needing to finish up inventory. Jason hated doing that kind of administrative stuff, so I wouldn't have to worry about him snooping. Bess shouldn't be out of the O.R. for at least an hour. It didn't leave me much time, but it would have to be enough.

I sent a quick text to Keara. "We need to step up delivery. Figure out a place to meet that's far away from the clinic. I'll meet you tonight."

Her answer was swift and decisive. She agreed. She gave me an address just outside of town.

I went back into the supply room. We had a pharmacy shipment coming in tomorrow. Near the end of the day already, I didn't have to worry about anyone needing things from back here. At best, we'd have some walk-ins needing heartworm pills and flea prevention.

I grabbed an empty box and straightened my back. No time to get squeamish now. I looted as many of the antibiotics as I could, leaving maybe a two-day supply in the cabinet. I arranged some of the other meds to make it look like the cabinet was more full than it was. My hands shook as I grabbed the vials of phenobarbital. It was the most potent drug we had, mostly used for euthanasia. Keara had a theory that in large enough quantities, it might work to incapacitate a shifter...at least for a little while. I prayed none of us would ever be in a position to test that theory.

Once I'd filled the box, I sealed it with packing tape. I'd leave it out in the alley by the dumpster, covering it with old newspapers.

Garbage pickup wasn't for two more days. I should be able to slip out and get it to my car before leaving for the day.

Testing the tape, I slid the box off the counter. The hallway was empty, so I stole outside unseen. I found a darkened corner near the dumpster and plenty of refuse to spread over the top of it. The goods would be safe and sound until I finished my shift. When I turned, I came face to face with Bess, standing in the doorway with her arms crossed.

My spine pricked as my brain went a million miles an hour. I tried to concentrate on keeping my breathing steady. We hadn't really discussed it, but I knew by instinct that Liam was tapped into my emotional state even more keenly since the other night. If he sensed me in distress, there's no telling what he might do.

I smoothed a hair out of my eyes and tried to muster the most normal smile I could. "Hey, Bess. Just trying to clean up the mess in the supply room. It got kind of out of hand. How did Dusty's cruciate repair go?"

She kept her hands crossed, her eyes darting over me. She was sweating beneath her lab coat and I didn't like the expression on her face.

"You've been with me a long time, Molly," she said. "Longer than Jason, even."

I moved away from the box by the dumpster, hoping desperately she hadn't seen too much. The dumpster itself was full to the brim. Pickup was tomorrow morning. It was plausible that I wouldn't have been able to fit the box inside of it. But, if she'd seen me covering it, I didn't know how to explain that away.

"I know," I said coming toward her. "Crazy, right?"

"Five years," she said. "I hired you right out of high school."

"Ha! Has it been that long? You thinking about throwing me a party? I'm sure Jason would be all over that. I think when he grows up he wants to be an event planner. He'd be great at it. The 2016 Christmas party is becoming the stuff of legends."

When I tried to go for the door, Bess moved, blocking my path. "What's in the box, Molly?"

My heart dropped. Fuck. She'd seen. "I told you." I figured I might as well commit. She was suspicious, but in the end, Bess had always been a pushover. "Expired stuff. Stuff we don't stock anymore. Garbage, mostly."

"There's a protocol for that," she said. "We don't just throw expired medication out in the trash."

She moved past me and headed for the dumpster. There was no point in trying to stop her. Bess leaned down, stuffed the newspapers in a corner and lifted the flap on the box. Her eyes darted over the contents and all color drained from her face.

Still squatting, she turned to me. Headlights flooded the alley. Bess's ride had arrived and my heart dropped.

"You gotta be kidding me," I said. It was too late to make a run for the baseball bat. Zeke stepped out of the driver's seat. His eyes hardened as he recognized me. The dent I'd put in the hood of his truck was still there.

"This is between us, Zeke," Bess said. "I'll be there in just a minute."

Zeke's jaw froze mid-chew. He had a wad of tobacco in his mouth. He let out breath and his mouth curved into a snarl. But, he climbed back into the cab of his truck, keeping the window rolled down.

Bess picked up the box of meds and walked it over to me. "What are you doing, Molly? You have to know how dangerous this is."

My gaze locked with hers. I could see everything she was thinking written plainly there. She knew.

"How long have you know about them?" I asked.

Bess's brow arched. "That's what you ask me? How long have I known? Come on, Molly. This is Shadow Springs. My father is a city councilman. My mother works in the mayor's office.

The Chief Pack is everywhere. That's what Liam told me when we first met. I just never realized how deep. I took a gamble. She'd either think I was crazy, or she wouldn't.

"Then you must know all of it. Have you seen what they do? How they force women to mate with shifters against their will? It's human trafficking, Bess. Do you support that?"

Pain crossed her face. She didn't think I was crazy. She looked back at Zeke to see if he was paying attention. At the moment, he was fiddling with the radio.

"Molly, this is dangerous, what you're doing. Never mind illegal. If you get caught…" She didn't finish the sentence. I couldn't bring myself to ask her whether she knew about the Langleys.

I grew bold. Stepping forward, I took the box from her. My heart started to beat again when she didn't try to keep it from me. She heaved it into my arms and took a step back.

"What do we do here, Bess?" I asked.

Her face went white as conflict swirled within her. Bess Kennedy had a big heart. It's what I liked most about her. I just prayed it would be the thing that kept her from standing in my way.

"No more," she whispered. "I mean it. I can't let you risk it. Those meds are assigned to *me*."

"Do you think I haven't thought of that? I've scraped off every serial and batch number. If anyone ever finds them, they won't be tied to you."

She spit out a laugh. "Jesus, Molly. You're not dumb. Don't act like it. How many veterinary clinics do you think there are in

Shadow Springs? We're it. Sure, it might not hold up in a court of law, but that's not what we're dealing with, is it?"

"Are you going to turn me in?" I asked. A pregnant pause hovered between us. Bess searched my face. Zeke's car door opened and he headed for us.

Bess plastered on a smile and turned to him. "Sorry, babe. We just had to go over some things so I don't forget tomorrow. We're about wrapped up now."

"Whatcha got in the box?" Zeke said. The smell of tobacco and liquor wafted off of him. Good God, he staggered when he walked. Was Bess actually thinking of letting him get behind the wheel like that with her in the car?

"Stool samples," I said pretending to foist it toward him. Zeke drew back. His eyes narrowed with contempt as he realized I'd just been joking.

"I'll take care of this," I said to Bess. "You two go on. I'll see you in the morning."

"You better watch yourself," Zeke said, stepping closer. "You've got a mouth on you. You're bossy. You do what Bess tells you, not the other way around."

"Hmm. I might say the same to you." God, I don't know why I didn't just smile and nod like some simpleton. I couldn't help it, Zeke brought out the worst in me.

"Molly," Bess warned. She put a hand on Zeke's arm and tried to pull him away. "Come on, baby. I'm hungry. You promised to take me to dinner."

He jerked his arm away from her and raised it. Bess's involuntary flinch seared through me. She took a few steps back, then turned, heading for the pickup. She'd abandoned me with Zeke.

He licked his lips and leered at me. My stomach rolled again. "I think you might need to start looking for another job. You know if you piss me off enough, I'll get her to fire you. Bess does what I say." Zeke got close enough that I could smell the beer on his breath.

A shadow crossed his face. My heart tripped and a hand came down, gripping Zeke's arm. Liam came from everywhere and nowhere. He pulled Zeke back and shoved him toward the pickup.

"Zeke, I think it's in your best interests to do what the fuck I say. Get in your car, drive away. Don't look back."

Zeke stumbled, but made his way back to the truck. Bess sat slack-jawed in the front seat. Zeke squealed the tires as he backed out and drove away.

Liam turned to me. "Come on. It's time to get you out of here."

FIFTEEN

LIAM

It was Molly's light touch on my arm that kept the wolf from coming out. It would have been so easy. I saw what she couldn't see. Zeke Redmond would hurt her. Angry lust poured through him as he looked at her, licking his lips. He wanted to control her, make her submit to him in the most degrading ways to punish her for standing up to him. My fingers trembled with the need to draw blood. My entire body emitted a low vibration as I stood between them.

Mercy. He would beg for it. I would show him none. But, Zeke got smart at the last second, knowing full well what I was. That was a different problem.

"I'm ready," Molly said. She stepped in my line of sight as Zeke's tires squealed and he drove away. She held a cardboard box in her arms, the sides bowed out from the weight of it. I took it from her.

"I brought my own truck this time," I said. She gave me a wide-eyed look.

"It's Keara's dad's," I said. "Or was. He passed away a couple of years ago. We don't use it much, but I figured it would be less conspicuous than me hauling you off over my shoulder."

A glimmer of desire made her eyes shine. It acted on me just like a drug. Lust poured through me and my cock was already hard just standing this close to her. I had to get a lid on it, fast. The Chief Pack was everywhere tonight. I'd passed two patrol cars on my way in. One of them slowed and gave me a curious look, but they didn't stop me. Word was, they were focusing on the Langley tragedy. If we were very lucky, they would think the trouble stopped with Brady.

God, my heart tore in two thinking about that poor kid.

"Did you see him?" Molly asked as she slid into the passenger seat. She was already getting so good at picking up my moods. She couldn't read my thoughts. Someday, if I ever marked her, she would. But pain sparked in her eyes that mirrored my own. Yes, I'd seen what they did to Brady, but I couldn't bring myself to tell her about it yet.

I'd parked the old Ford pickup one street over. I leaned forward and locked her seatbelt. She gave me a wry smile.

"Sorry," I said. "I just want to make sure you're safe."

She leaned in and gave me a chaste kiss on the lips. Well, I think she meant it that way at any rate. Just that light touch stirred my wolf. We had only just begun the other night. I had so many more things I wanted to do to her if we ever got the chance.

"I'm safe," she said. "For now."

I started to drive out of town, happy to put some distance between us and the clinic. It had gotten so I could barely stand pavement beneath my feet or walls surrounding me. I needed the open air and the woods. I knew what that could mean. With each passing day, more of my wildness took root. It was like that for all of us. Well, some of us. Molly kept me tethered to the tamer parts of my nature. Keara did the same for Jagger. For Mac, Gunnar, and Payne, I worried the most. The more feral we went, the easier it would be for the Pack to track us down.

"What was that back there?" She knew I'd evaded her question about Brady and let it go for now. Now it was her turn to be evasive.

"It was nothing," she said. "Nothing I couldn't handle, anyway."

I turned off the highway. In another mile, we'd reach the edge of the woods and would have to go the rest of the way on foot. I had a plan to conceal the truck beneath some fallen branches.

"Molly, it's no good. You've got to be straight with me. I'll be able to tell if you're not."

Her heartbeat quickened. I put a hand over hers to calm her. Then, I drew her palm to my lips and kissed her. I loved how just that little touch sent gooseflesh straight up her arm.

"Bess knows," she sighed. "I don't know how deep her knowledge goes, but she knows. She's got family in local government."

I dropped Molly's hand in my lap. Keeping my eyes on the road, I nodded. The Chief Pack had Shadow Springs on lock. It had been that way for over fifty years. The mayor himself was one of the Alpha's strongest enforcers. He wasn't in charge though. We'd been trying to root out his top general for months. Jagger had a theory that if we took him out, we might punch a dent into the Pack's hold on Shadow Springs. He hadn't yet told Keara about the plan. Evading the Pack and stockpiling supplies was one thing. Going on the offensive was something altogether different.

"Then I don't want you going back there. I'm serious, Molly. We can't trust anyone."

She tapped her fingers against the dashboard. "Normally, I'd agree with you. I don't know though. She let me leave with the meds, Liam. She didn't have to. Hell, she could have called the police then and there. She knows it's her neck in the noose if anyone figures out what I stole."

I parked the car down a shallow embankment right before the woods got deep. Stepping out, I came around and helped Molly down. It took ten seconds to camouflage the car, then I took her hand and led her toward the cave entrance. Each step of the way, I stalled for time. I didn't like the risk she'd taken one bit. Bess Kennedy was weak. She couldn't be trusted. If I had my way, Molly would never leave the caves again. Though I knew that wasn't fair. There was also no way Jagger and the others would allow it. Not yet.

Once we'd made it through the steepest of the passageways but before branching off to the encampment, I turned to her. I found a lantern we kept near the wall and flicked it on. Molly's face glowed in the dim light. Her beautiful, brown eyes searched my face. I had to touch her. I had to have the feel of her skin against mine. How I'd made it more than a day without seeing her I don't know.

"I know what you want to ask me," she said, giving me a soulful smile.

"Yeah? How's that?" We had just these few stolen moments before the others would come. I promised the others I wouldn't try to mark her. I wouldn't put the others at risk or her. But, now that I had her close to me again and her gaze met mine, I knew I was a fool. Jagger was right. This was too damn hard.

"How much time do we have?" she whispered. My little Molly was too smart by half.

"Not long. Keara convinced them to let us have the night. In the morning, some decisions have to be made."

"About me?" she took a step back, her eyes filled with despair.

"About a lot of things."

"Liam." My name ripped from her throat. She came to me, sliding her hands up my chest. "For now I just want to be where you are. It...hurts when I'm not."

My heart split in two. It seemed I was destined to live that way the moment I set eyes on this woman. "I don't want to hurt you. I want to keep you safe. We just have to figure out the best way to do that."

Molly pulled away. Smiling, she ran a hand through her hair. "And it sounds like the others have decided that's all going to happen by a committee vote, I take it. I'm not sure how I feel about that."

"Come on," I said. "The committee can wait. I want to hear more about what happened with Bess."

Trusting, she took my hand. I led her down the smooth passageways, deeper underground. Her steps were surer this time. Though she'd only been down to the caves a couple of times now, she was starting to find her way by instinct.

We reached the cavern where I slept most nights. Molly went inside hugging her arms. She blew a hair out of her face and looked up.

"We're below my trailer, aren't we?"

I stayed against the wall by the mouth of the cavern, watching her. "How did you know?"

"I could feel it. I could feel you. But Liam, I don't understand it. You came here before you even met me."

"I know." It was really the only answer I could give her. It wasn't enough. I just knew what I felt.

"Fate. That word Keara keeps using. And the mark on her neck. I wanted you to bite me. Liam, I wanted it so badly. I still want it now."

She wasn't asking me. Not yet. But God, just the mention of the mark. I didn't know if I could be strong enough to deny her.

"I can't," I said, hating myself for it. "We can't. Not now. Molly, if I mark you, it's forever. At least as long as we're both alive. It would bind you to me in a way that would make you a target. If the Chief Pack figured it out, they could use you against me."

"I would *never* betray you!" Molly's eyes flashed with fury.

I went to her. I put gentle arms around her. "Of course you wouldn't. But they'd hurt you knowing I could feel it. Knowing I'd come for you no matter what. And if it came to a choice…" I couldn't complete the thought. Molly did it for me.

"If it came to a choice, you'd choose me over the others. If you thought you could end whatever suffering the Pack put me through, you'd do it."

I swallowed hard, letting the look in my eyes be her answer. She reached up and ran her fingers over my cheekbone.

"Then, we can't," she said. "No matter how hard it is, you can't mark me."

My wolf raged to the surface. Molly saw it in my eyes. I couldn't take it. I went to the wall and punched it. Blood flowed between my knuckles. It took the edge off the anger welling inside of me.

Molly stayed stock still against the opposite wall, waiting for my temper to ease. Then, she came to me. "But we can…we can be together like we were the other night. Can't we? Because Liam, I don't think I can bear not to."

"Come here," I said. I took her by the hand and led her to the pallet I kept on the ledge on the far side of the cave. She deserved so much more. She deserved satin sheets with roses on them, champagne and bubble baths. She deserved all the things I couldn't give her.

"I just want you," she said, again, proving how connected we already were to each other's moods. It thrilled me and scared me all at once. I hadn't told her the whole truth. No, I hadn't fully marked or claimed her. But, the bond we already shared might be too strong for either of us to turn away from.

"Tell me your dreams, Molly," I said. "You already know mine."

"Do I?"

I leaned back and pulled her against me. She fit perfectly in the hollow beneath my shoulder. I smoothed her hair back as she looked up at me.

"I want to find a way to get out from under the Chief Pack once and for all. I want us to live freely. Far from here if we have to."

"Is there a place? I mean, if you were able to get far enough away?"

I shrugged. "We'd be hunted forever. If we were betas, maybe. We'd pose no threat to other packs in other territories. I think I told you that. But, I think maybe I'd like to try. I think maybe I have a good enough reason to take the risk. There are packs in the north near the Canadian border and through the Upper Peninsula of Michigan. They might be willing to help us. If we could find a way to get there."

"Would you take me with you?" I looked at her. From the expression on her face, I couldn't tell if she were asking for herself or just to know my plans. Before I could ask her, she changed the subject.

"Is there a way to defeat him?" she asked. "The Alpha. Keara said he's older than any Alpha anyone's ever known. She said she thinks the secret is what he draws from the Pack members he controls."

"I think that's true. But no one except his most trusted generals can get close to him. He's surrounded by lethal Pack soldiers all the time. He keeps them feral. Makes them kill for him. They've been in their wolves so long, I don't even know if they have any trace of their human selves left."

"God, that sounds awful. They must be in agony. I wish there were some way to help them."

My Molly. Sweet Molly. Of course she would think of mercy when I could only think of death. Because to live like that would be hell. The only release I could think of was to kill them before they hurt someone I cared about.

Her face darkened as she turned my words over in her mind. "Liam," she asked. "Isn't there some way to at least weaken their hold on the Pack? I mean, you keep talking about these generals. What happens if you take one of them out?"

She read the answer in my face. Her breath hitched. "That's what Keara's really planning for, isn't it? There might come a day when you can *never* go topside."

I smoothed the hair from her face. "We take it one day at a time. What about you, my love?" I said. She stiffened at the word, then settled back against me. "I asked you to tell me your dreams."

She smiled up at me. "Well, they've changed a bit over the last few weeks. But, I'd like to be able to go back to school. I was saving up to get my D.V.M. Bess even hinted at helping me with that before...before all this. She said she wanted me to be her partner. Now, I just wonder…"

"Wonder what?"

A crease formed between Molly's eyes. I recognized it now as one of her tells. She was having a stubborn thought. "What the Alpha's doing to that pack. It's not natural. If you hadn't told me that yourself, I can sense it now. Those firefighters at the Langleys, they were...odd...like they weren't thinking for themselves. They couldn't make a move without getting some sort of telepathic order. I'd love to study one of them. You know, like in a lab."

Molly's mind was a marvel as well as her body. She was my fated mate, but I would have fallen in love with her anyway. And so I told her.

"I love you," I said. "It's selfish of me to say it considering what we're up against. But there it is."

Molly wrinkled her nose and smiled. The blush I was growing to love so much colored her cheeks. "I was kind of thinking that too. You know...that you love me."

Laughing, I reached for her and pinched her ass. Not hard enough to cause her pain, but hard enough that she squealed. The sound of it worked on me like a drug, waking my wolf. God, would I ever be able to be near this woman without wanting to fuck her? Part of me hoped not.

"When?" she gasped.

"What do you mean?"

"When does the committee meet?"

"Baby, it's not really a committee."

Molly snorted. "I know that. But you're not a pack. I don't know what else to call you."

"Fair point. And I'm not sure. We have some time."

The heat poured off of her. A fuse ignited inside of me as Molly moved away from me. She stood and slowly lifted the hem of her shirt. Kicking off her shoes, she wriggled out of her scrub bottoms. She was only wearing a bra and panties underneath. She cast a nervous glance over her shoulder.

"We're alone," I said, barely able to get the words out. My wolf raged. I was rock hard already. Molly reached back and unsnapped her bra. Her little striptease damn near ended me and she knew it. She flashed me a devilish smile as she dragged her panties down.

I made a move toward her and she put a hand up to stop me. "I've been wanting to do this for a while," she whispered. She unzipped my jeans and dragged them down. My cock sprung out huge and hard.

Tilting her head to the side, she gathered her hair and pushed it behind her shoulder. With her eyes fixed on mine, she slid her lips over the tip, swirling her tongue up and down the shaft of my cock.

"Oh, God," I gasped, throwing my head back. I loved her all over again.

Molly circled her fingers around the base of my cock, stroking me there while she worked her magic with her mouth. When she used her free hand to massage my balls I damn near lost my mind.

The other night, I had been the one to draw her to the edge and bring her back. Now, Molly took control. I gripped the stone ledge, feeling strong enough to crumble it to powder. Molly worked quickly, skillfully, bringing me to the edge, then drawing back. She was perfect. Gorgeous. Mine.

When she increased her pace, I couldn't hold back. It became clear she didn't want me to. Growling loud enough to echo through the cave, I came. Molly redoubled her efforts, working her jaw to keep up with me. I spilled my seed inside of her and she took in every drop.

When I was spent, I couldn't feel my legs anymore. But, it only lasted a second. When Molly rose, my hands went up. I traced her curves, loving the way her supple flesh twitched beneath my fingertips. I caught her nipples between my thumbs and forefingers and gently rolled them. Molly threw her head back, swaying on the balls of her feet. I sat up, sliding my hands between her thighs. I made her part them for me.

"Liam," she gasped. "I can't."

"Oh, yes, you can, baby," I said, my voice a wicked whisper.

With two fingers I spread open her velvety folds. One quick dart of my tongue over her sensitive little bud made her scream with pleasure. I used one hand to hold her up. Her knees quivered so much I thought she might lose her balance. But, once I settled my mouth on the task at hand, Molly threw her head back and undulated with me.

She tasted like the sweetest honey. Her juices flowed and her tiny clit grew rock hard as I sucked her there. I fucked her with my tongue and she couldn't hold on a second longer. I didn't want her to.

"Liam!" she cried out. I knew the others were close enough to hear her, of course, but they kept their distance.

Molly carved her fingers through my hair, drawing me down on her even deeper. She spread open for me, each wave of her orgasm twitching against my tongue. I drank her all in. It was just the beginning. I wanted to do so much more. I wished we had all the time in the world. I would cherish her in ways she'd never dreamt before. But this would have to be enough.

As Molly crested down, I showed her mercy, releasing the suction. She let out a sigh and sank into me, boneless. I carried her down. Curving her body against mine, Molly let me hold her in my lap. I placed sweet kisses on each of her breasts.

"I love you too," she said, her eyes wet with tears. "God help us both, Liam. I love you too."

SIXTEEN

LIAM

L ater, we faced the others. My heart split watching Molly walk straight-backed into the rotunda. She held my hand tightly.

Jagger stood with his back to us in the corner of the cavern. Mac, Payne, and Gunnar sat on a ledge near him looking grim. Only Keara came to Molly. With sad eyes, she took Molly's hands in hers and hugged her.

"What do we know?" I asked. I knew the others had things to say to me about Molly, but I was in no mood to hear them. Especially not with her standing right there.

"We're not sure," Mac said. "One of our contacts said a few of the Pack members went to the Langleys' store the morning of the fire. He doesn't know what was said. But Liam, they left. They didn't try to take Brady with them."

"Do you think Bernie did this himself?" Molly asked, horrified.

"No," Jagger said, his voice snapping. "No. Bernie was a lot of things, but he never would have killed Brady. Himself, maybe.

But he wouldn't have done something that would have gotten Ellie or Brady hurt.

"Then we have to assume the worst," I said. "Bernie and Ellie got made. This was our fault."

"But why?" Molly said, tearing her hands from Keara and turning to face the others. "So fine, Bernie and Ellie I understand, horrifying as it is. The Chief Pack wanted to send a message. This is what happens to anyone who tries to resist. But why kill Brady too? Why wouldn't they have just hauled him off to report like he was supposed to anyway?"

"Because they knew he was defective," Keara said, choking back a sob. "Molly you saw him. His bones broke every day. This wasn't retaliation. It was an extermination. And it means they're getting bolder."

"So now what?" Payne asked. He started to pace. His wolf eyes flashed.

"Now we fight just as hard," Molly said.

"No! You've done enough."

"No, she hasn't!" Jagger shouted it. "We need Molly and that doctor now more than ever, and you know it. We need eyes and ears up there. You've brought her into this, Liam; it's too late to back out now."

"It's okay," Molly said. "I'll be smart. No more drops. And Bess Kennedy knows something. She could have stopped me from bringing those meds to you today, but she didn't. She helped us. She has connections in higher places than you've had access to before. I'll be careful. I'll lay low. But we carry on. I'm in this with you now, like it or not."

Jagger turned on me. He couldn't hide the hint of a smile. I wanted to rip his face off. "If I haven't said it before," his voice boomed across the cavern walls. "I like her, Liam."

SEVENTEEN

MOLLY

I went on autopilot for the next few days. Though it had been my choice, leaving Liam and the others behind felt like I'd ripped out a part of my soul and left it with them. But, I knew in my heart it was necessary. With everything that had happened at the Langleys' store, being topside had become increasingly dangerous for them. Liam needed me to be his eyes and ears in Shadow Springs whether either of us liked it or not.

The clinic stayed busy, and I found myself avoiding Bess and sticking to conversations only related to office matters. To her credit, she did the same. Until the day she didn't.

At the end of the day, the week after I last left Liam, Bess found me while I was finishing up charting for the day. She came into the office and quietly shut the door. Everyone else had left, so it was just the two of us.

Bess stood with her back against the door. She chewed her bottom lip and made a few false starts with heavy breaths before she finally said what she'd come for. I stayed stone still, my pen poised above a pad of paper.

"Is it enough?" she said.

I waited a beat, then leaned back in the chair, tossing the pen to the desk. "Is what enough, Bess?"

With slow, halting steps, she came forward and eased herself into one of the chairs on the other side of the desk. It was a strange dynamic, me sitting behind *her* desk with her on the opposite side...as if I were the doctor and she was the patient.

She folded her hands and rested them on the desk. Leaning in, she spoke so quietly I had to strain to hear. It made my spine prickle. We were the only two people in the building. "For your friends," she said. "Was the package you took them enough?"

I felt like I had quicksand under my feet. Alarm bells went off. She'd helped me. There was no doubt of it. But, could I trust her? I realized this had to have been the same sensation Keara must have had when Liam brought me to the caves for the first time.

I had a choice to make. In the span of a heartbeat, I made it. "No. Of course it isn't enough. As long as things remain...how they are...it will never be enough, Bess."

Her face fell. She slowly closed her eyes and sat back in her chair. When she opened them again, they were bloodshot with the first hint of fresh tears. "You don't know how dangerous this is for me," she said.

"I think I do. And I also think your conscience is telling you we have to find a way to do more." I paused, took a steadying breath, then dove in with both feet.

"Bess, you know what happened to Bernie and Ellie Langley. And you know why it happened."

She ran a hand through her hair. "And I know it's going to *keep* happening."

"Exactly. So help me. The Chief Pack is getting bolder. More people are going to get hurt or disappear just like the Langleys if people like you and me don't step up and do the right thing."

A tear slid down her cheek. "We're the ones who will disappear, Molly. Don't you get it? There's too many of them. They've been in power too long. And don't start lecturing me. You're the one who is new to this. Not me. My father, the people who run this town. The Pack is entrenched. You've only now woken up to it. I've lived it my whole life."

"What do you mean?"

Bess brought trembling fingers to her mouth. She squeezed her eyes shut and let the rest of her tears fall. "My father tried to stand up to the Alpha when I was a little girl. Every year, he'd take more and more. Installing Pack members in positions of power. There were payoffs, kickbacks. Everything in this town has been engineered so the Chief Pack has all the money and security they need. My father saw it happening. He's a good man. Honest. But, he paid Molly. They...they made my *brother* disappear. He was twelve years old."

My heart went cold. "Oh. God. Oh, Bess. I had no idea."

She fixed her sad eyes on me and my heart broke for her. "You have no idea how far the Alpha's reach is. No idea. Your friends are fooling themselves."

I leaned forward. "But you're going to help me help them anyway."

Bess fixed her eyes on a point over my shoulder. She shook her head then looked back at me. "If they ever find out…"

"They won't. I've been careful enough so far."

She gave me a hollow smile. "That's what everyone says."

I came around the desk and put my arms around her. "You're doing the right thing, Bess. We both know it."

Bess squeezed me back. I felt strength in her I hadn't seen before. I loved her a little bit for it.

"Give me a few days," she said, sighing. "I have a couple of ideas."

My heart was full. I hugged her one last time then left her alone.

————

Bess's plan came in the form of a visit she arranged just two days later. Jason called me back for a tech visit. Nothing major, just a tabby needing her claws trimmed. It was the odd look on Bess's face when I brushed past her that made me bristle.

When I opened the door to Exam Room Two, my heart burst.

"Keara!" I shouted a whisper and slammed the door behind me. Keara met me with a bright smile and open arms.

I sat on the bench next to her, beaming. She'd been near Liam, recently. I could catch his scent lingering in the air and it startled me. But, Keara understood.

"It's going to be like that forever," she said. "And even more intense if you ever...if he…"

"If he marks me," I said. "We've talked about it."

Her expression went instantly grave. "I would love to take the high road here and say it's none of my business, but you know it is. And I also realize the kind of hypocrite it makes me for cautioning you to be careful with it."

I touched her shoulder. "It doesn't make you a hypocrite. It makes you wise. You know I put a lot of stock in your advice. But, that's not why you're here."

She cast a furtive glance toward the exam room door. "No, it's not.

I took a chance coming here. Your vet friend found me. Did you know that?"

"She's more than a friend, I think. Bess might be an important ally."

Keara stood up. She grew restless, not quite knowing what to do with her hands.

"How is he?" I asked. I couldn't pretend. To her credit, Keara didn't torture me with half-truths and evasion.

"He's terrible, Molly. I've never seen Liam like this. He's bouncing off the damn cave walls all the time. Jagger and the others don't know what to do with him."

"He's not taking chances he shouldn't, is he?" My heart thundered. In some ways, I felt like a junior high school girl asking for news about her boyfriend. Except being away from him was tearing me up in every way.

"No," Keara answered straight. "Liam's smart. I'll never admit I said this, but he's smarter than Jagger. The caves were Liam's idea. A few years ago, we'd heard a rumor that another exiled pack from Michigan had been using them to hide out in. That pack is all dead now. Liam did all the recon."

She was babbling. It made me uneasy because it wasn't like her. Something was wrong. She also wouldn't have come here just for a social visit.

"Keara," I said. "You have to tell me what's happening. It's killing me to be out of the loop. You of all people should understand why."

She finally stopped pacing and rounded on me. "I'm sorry. You're right. We're in trouble, Molly."

"Oh, God, please don't tell me the Pack has found you."

"No. God, no. Not yet. It's kind of the opposite. Since the tragedy with the Langleys, most of our topside allies have gotten spooked. Some have just cut off all contact out of fear. Molly, I'm worried about supplies. Jagger, Liam, the others...they can't hunt right now. It's too dangerous. We have enough food stores down there to last a few months at best. Or at least we did...but...those who haven't cut and run, well, they're asking for sanctuary. In the last week, we've taken in twenty refugees. Eight shifters and some of their non-shifter families. Plus a few of our other suppliers who've gotten too scared of getting caught."

My heart sank. "And you don't have enough to feed and clothe them all. Never mind medical needs when they arise."

Keara let out a sob that ripped through me. I'd never seen her cry. I'd never even seen her upset. It occurred to me that she probably had to keep up a brave front to keep the others from breaking down. I went to her, putting my arms around her.

"I'm sorry," she snorted. "This is embarrassing."

"Don't be. Keara, you're shouldering a lot. My God, it's amazing really. Think of how many lives you've saved."

She pulled away. "Saved? Molly, I can't stop thinking of how many lives I've put in jeopardy. I'm not ready for this. We're not ready for this. In a year, maybe. Once I've established a more solid network and stockpile. I don't know what happened. Somebody got to the Langleys. I've gone over it and over it. We were so careful. I can't figure out who betrayed them."

"Maybe no one," I said. "We'll never know what happened in that store. Maybe they finally just came for Brady and Bernie put up a fight he couldn't win. There's no sense in beating yourself up over it."

She sniffled and nodded. "I know you're right. It just gets so hard sometimes. Everyone looks to me for answers. Even Jagger. I'm just doing the best that I can. I feel so alone sometimes."

I put a solid grip on her shoulders and looked her in the eye. "You're not. You hear me? You're not. I'm here too. I'm not going anywhere. And now we have Bess."

Keara's eyes widened. "You're sure?"

"Yes. Give me time. For the moment, I think we can at least trust her to help get more medical supplies. But, she has a reason to want to bring the Chief Pack down. I can't go into it all now. You should get back. Bess has connections though. Give me a few days to work on her. I've got a few ideas."

Keara's smile deepened. It looked like a physical weight lifted from her shoulders, and I was so happy to play a part in it. She hugged me in earnest.

"You're good at this, you know," she said. "You're a natural."

"Good at what?"

"Recruiting. You have a way about you. I'm not surprised your Bess is willing to put herself out there for you."

"Well, like I said. She's got reasons of her own."

The intercom buzzed. It was Jason calling me back to the front desk.

"Come on," I said. "Let's slip you out the back."

"Do you have anything you want me to take back for you? A message maybe?"

Keara's eyes danced with mischief. God, how I wished we could just be normal girlfriends gossiping over a cup of coffee. I had the strange sensation things could never be normal again. Stranger still, I wasn't sure I ever wanted them to be.

"Just tell Liam to stay safe."

She hugged me. "Funny, that's the only thing he could come up with for me to tell you."

"Let's arrange to meet. Do you know where my trailer is? If not, Liam can show you. I think it's probably safer there than here. Like I said. Give me two or three days. I'll find a way to get more supplies. Start coming up with a list of what you need."

That devilish smirk came in Keara's eyes again. She reached into her back pocket and produced a folded piece of paper. She thrust it in my hand. "I knew I'd be able to count on you."

"Great," I laughed. "And you say *I'm* good at this. Okay. Two days. Meet me at Shady Acres about an hour after my shift ends. Eight o'clock. You think you can keep those dogs on a leash until then?"

Keara rolled her eyes. "They sure are something, aren't they?"

I opened the back door and peered into the alley. The coast was clear. My heart hardened as Keara stepped outside. She wasn't Liam, of course, but she was a vital link to him. I just wasn't sure how long I could go without seeing him. Just sensing him below me, miles underground, was torture. As Keara left, I decided I wouldn't go much longer at all. I needed to find a way to see him.

Bess was waiting for me when I came back inside. She had a hard stare that made my stomach flip. For an instant, I worried she'd changed her mind about all of it. But, her hand on my arm put that to rest.

"Tell me what you need and when," she said, smiling.

EIGHTEEN

MOLLY

Once Bess put her mind to helping me, she was a dynamo. How she did it, I'll never know. It occurred to me it was better I didn't. But within forty-eight hours, she'd procured enough medical supplies to outfit a second clinic.

"You sure about all of this?" I asked her.

"No." Bess stood in the alley with her hands on her hips. "I think I can do better."

"This is plenty for now. We need to pace ourselves."

"You sure you don't want me to come with you?" she asked. "How are you planning on carrying all of this stuff?"

I curled my bicep and kissed it, teasing her. "Let's just say I have unusually strong friends."

"Right. You know, the minute I saw that guy in the alley, I knew he'd be all over you."

My heart tripped. It's the first time we'd really talked about that first night when Liam showed up. I went to her.

"You sure you're okay with this? I know the risk you're taking."

Before I could say another word, Bess put a hand up to stop me. "Don't. Believe me, I wouldn't be doing this if I didn't want to. I more than anyone know about risk. I just hope it gets put to good use and helps."

"It will. You have no idea." I got a little choked up. Bess Kennedy had frustrated me to no end over the years. But, she was a friend and always had been. Never more so than now.

"Just do me a favor," she said, giving me a hollow smile.

"Anything, you know it."

"Just tell your unusually strong friends to save some room for me wherever these supplies are going. I have a feeling I might need it someday."

I hugged her again. I answered her promise with a nod. Nothing more needed to be said.

It was already half past seven. Keara would be prompt. Excitement fluttered in my gut as I slammed the lid on my trunk and slid into the driver's seat. Bess had no idea how much she'd helped. Nothing would ever make up for the loss of Brady and the Langleys, but this was at least a solid start.

The moon rose low in the sky as I headed to the outskirts of town. Mammoth Forest loomed large and the tang of pine filled my nostrils. Liam was out there somewhere. Watching. Waiting. Soon, I'd have a decision to make. It had been a half-innocent comment, almost a joke on Bess's part, but a deeper truth rang through it.

The time would come when it wouldn't be safe for me to stay above ground either. I trusted Bess, but I couldn't trust those around her. As strong as she'd been to help me this far, I couldn't trust her with my life...not yet.

As I made the turn into the trailer park, my skin pricked. I hadn't realized I'd been on the precipice of a decision, but once I'd made it, I knew it was right.

I wouldn't be going back to the clinic after this. I would follow Keara back to the caves and stay there. The pull to Liam was far too strong. And as confident as Bess was about what she'd done, there was no way the disappearance of this amount of meds wouldn't raise questions somewhere.

The moment I'd made the decision, my heart soared. I would see Liam again. Tonight.

I could barely contain myself as I took the last winding road leading to the back of the trailer park. I passed Lisa. She sat on her front porch with tonight's date and waved as I went by. I didn't wave back. I was too keyed up.

Keara waited on the front porch. I cut the engine and got out. Keara's bright smile helped settle my nerves. I motioned for her and popped the trunk. Keara's eyes grew wide when she saw. My entire backseat and trunk were filled to the brim with cardboard boxes.

"This is all medicine?" she gasped.

"No," I answered. "I mean, about half of it is. I also picked up some foodstuffs from the wholesale food place. We're not talking a year supply or anything, but I figured every little bit will help."

Keara hugged me. "It will, my God. You have no idea how much."

When she pulled away, she read something in my eyes. "What is it?"

Shrugging, I leaned against the car. "I'm coming with you," I told her. "It's time."

"Molly."

"Don't try to talk me out of it. I need you on my side. Liam's going to put up a fight. I mean, not so much Liam. But Jagger and the others will. That is...unless you can convince them otherwise."

Her expression softened. "I'm selfish, you know. It's a hundred percent safer for you to stay here, keep working at the clinic. But, I won't deny the idea of having a true friend who's not...well...furry in her off hours is tremendously tempting."

I laughed. "Shows how much you know. Give me a day without a razor and then we'll talk."

"You're sure though. I mean *really* sure?"

"Yes." I put a hand on her shoulder. "I'm miserable without him. And it's only a matter of time. Bess has been a good friend, but I can't trust her all the way. She doesn't have the best judgment."

"You haven't told her about this?" Keara asked.

"About the caves? Oh, good God, no. It's better if I'm just gone."

I felt a pang of doubt when I said it. It wasn't Bess that I worried about leaving. The thought of not even getting to say goodbye to Jason and Michael stung though. Hot tears stung my eyes.

Keara understood. She'd made the same choice herself not long ago. She drew me into a hug again. When she let go, my heart raced with excitement. Hard as it might be, I'd made up my mind and Keara supported my decision. I hadn't realized how much I'd worried about her reaction. A thrill went through me. I was keyed up again and eager to get moving.

Maybe that's why I didn't hear the truck behind me. Or maybe it's why I didn't fully register the change in Keara's expression. The flood of headlights hit her and she shielded her eyes against them. Keara's eyes widened with fear I couldn't understand. She shouted a warning, but it was as if no sound came out.

I turned. That's when I saw the pickup. Zeke was driving. He cut his engine and got out. Except this time he wasn't alone.

Before I could even react, three other men poured out of Zeke's truck. He sat there behind the wheel grinning with menace as his companions surrounded us. One of them went straight for Keara. He cut off her scream with an elbow to the face.

It happened so fast. The other two men got to me. One put a hand on my shoulder and forced me to the ground. They were so big. So strong. So deadly. I recognized one as Tenley, the volunteer fireman from the other night.

Behind me, Keara did find the strength to scream. But, that's the last thing I heard before the lights went out.

NINETEEN

LIAM

W e are not pack. We are not connected in that way. But, when agony ripped through Jagger, each one of us felt it.

He dropped to his knees and his wolf ripped out of him. Payne and Gunnar were closest. Jagger's wolf bared his teeth and turned on them. His eyes blazed, not silver as they usually did, but red.

At first, I thought the Alpha had somehow taken hold of his mind again. Panic stirred me and my own wolf chafed to get out. Mac nearly shifted himself. He stood furthest down the path. We'd been clearing debris to make a new passageway. Keara wanted smaller caverns ready to accommodate our growing number of refugees. We took in more every day.

"Jagger!" Gunnar was closest. He squared off with Jagger's wolf. I could feel his own need to shift coursing through him. I shuddered and gripped the cave walls, drawing blood as my claws came out.

Jagger's howl turned to a yelp of pain that struck me through the heart. This wasn't the Alpha. This was Keara.

"Shit!" I yelled, sensing Jagger's move before he made it. He couldn't stop himself. This pull was more powerful than anything the Alpha could do. His mate was in trouble...oh, God. She was in pain. "Get hold of him!"

Jagger had just enough man inside of him to understand my words. He turned on me, fangs bared, saliva dripping from them. The message was clear. He'd kill me...he'd kill any of us to get to Keara if that's what it took. If I ever doubted that I'd do the same for Molly when the time came, Jagger's bloodlust made that clear.

Wolf on man, he would tear me apart. But, if I gave into the beast, one of us would die. Gunnar, Payne, and Mac acted together. Thank God for them. While Jagger's attention was focused on me, each of them shifted. They pounced on Jagger, throwing him against the wall with enough force to crack his ribs.

But Jagger was a man possessed. I died a little inside that day. A year ago, we all knew it might come to this. If Jagger's pull to Keara ever jeopardized the rest of us, we'd made an unspoken pact to stop him.

And stop him we did. Even in his crazed state, Jagger's wolf was no match for all three of them. My own wolf jittering through me, I straightened my back and went to him. They had Jagger pinned to the ground. He snarled and snapped, but he couldn't break free.

I leaned down, getting close enough that he could see my eyes, but not close enough that he could rip my face off.

"Jagger," I said. "We need you human, man. *She* needs you human. We'll figure out what to do."

Jagger howled, but his eyes faded from red to pink to silver, then finally a calmer blue. Though he struggled against the weight of the others, he let out a heaving sigh and shifted back. Sweat covered his body. Payne's claws ripped into his shoulder.

"Ease up," I said. "He can't talk if he can't breathe."

Payne and Gunnar shifted back to human. Only Mac stayed in his wolf.

"Let me go," Jagger said, his voice ragged with pain. "They're going to kill her. She's terrified."

"What do you see?"

Jagger's eyelids fluttered. His breathing came in uneven pants. When he snapped them open, the bloodlust returned for a fraction of a second. Then, he focused on me.

"They tricked her," he said. Icy fear coiled through my gut. It was as if I knew what he was going to say before he said it.

"Keara was going up to pick up a supply shipment," Payne said. He moved, still wedging his knee into Jagger's shoulder, giving him more room to breathe.

"Three of them," Jagger said. He strained against Payne and Gunnar's weight. Mac's wolf snarled behind him.

"The three that chased Molly and me the other night." It was a statement, not a question. I knew in my heart it was true. I'd been so caught up in Jagger's distress, I missed the faint pulse of my own. I focused on breathing.

Mac sensed it rising in me. We are not pack, but he is my brother. If he'd followed the others and shifted back, things might have ended differently. But, he didn't. Mac's wolf acted with lightning quickness. He backed me into a corner. His low growl an echoing threat through the cavern. I put my palms out in surrender.

"Three of them," Jagger said again. "They took them."

Them. They took them. I closed my eyes and tried to still my rumbling wolf. I had to think. The miles of rock above our heads had provided us with protection. Now, they kept me from feeling what I needed to feel. Molly was mine, but I hadn't marked her. I couldn't sense her as an extension of myself yet. Not the way Jagger did with Keara. Maybe it kept me sane for a few moments longer. But in the end, my mind went numb anyway as Jagger's words seemed to hover in the air then finally land.

"Molly and Keara. Let me go or kill me. It's the only way you're going to keep me from trying to get to her," he said.

My eyes snapped open. "No. You're not dying today."

"Goddammit!" Jagger struggled against Payne and Gunnar.

I put a hand up and locked eyes with Mac's wolf. "Stand down," I told him. "I'm not going to do anything stupid." That was partly a lie. But, at least I'd try to protect the rest of them along with the girls. Jagger was too far gone.

Mac didn't shift, but his wolf dropped his head. He took two steps back, giving me some room.

"Jagger, we can't," Payne said. He ran a hand across his jaw. Keeping Jagger immobile was tearing them apart. He would hate us for it. I hated us for it.

"Let me go," I said.

"No," Gunnar said. "God, we've talked about this. We all know the risks. Jagger goes topside for even thirty seconds, the Pack's going to sense him. The way he is now, they'll be able to track him. It's not safe."

"If you let her die, it won't matter," Jagger said, his voice flat.

"Jagger," I got in his face. "They have Molly too. If someone led the Pack to her, I have a pretty good idea who that might have been. I can track Bess Kennedy. It won't take long, I've been around her enough. I can get to her faster than any of us. You have to trust me."

"We don't *need* Bess Kennedy," Jagger spat. "You think I can't track Keara myself? I know exactly where she is. I see what she sees. And right now, it's dark, Jagger. So, so dark. She's hurt. But she's in a warehouse just off the interstate. Five miles south."

"I know it," Gunnar said.

"We can't go charging in there like this," Payne said. "You know this is killing me as much as the rest of you. But this is what they *want* us to do. It's what they expect."

"We need intel," I said. "We need to know how many are with her. Who's guarding them. Bess might know that. If she's the one who tipped the pack off, I can work with that. I can persuade her."

I hated the sound of my own voice and what I was suggesting. Bess Kennedy was used to being victimized. God, I hoped I could appeal to her in another way. But, the thought of Molly and Keara being at the mercy of the Pack tore my guts apart.

"Go," Jagger said. "Go now."

I didn't wait for the others. I ran. The moment I emerged from the caves, Molly's scent filled me. Jagger was exactly right about where she was. Instinct fueled me, pushing me toward her. I had to leave my heart behind and head in the opposite direction.

TWENTY

Liam

Bess Kennedy lived in a tiny brick house on the east side of town. A well-manicured, tree lined street. Quiet. Affluent. It would be easy to pretend here that nothing sinister lurked in the woods beyond.

Tonight, I was that sinister thing.

I wondered later if she had been waiting for me. I found her sitting quietly on her back porch. The cool autumn air blew through her auburn hair. She was already crying when I got there.

I clenched my fists at my sides. The wolf burned strong within me. With each heartbeat, I felt Molly slipping further away from me. She was shutting down. Trying to stay calm. Even now, she was trying to protect me.

I didn't wait for an invitation. I walked up Bess's freshly cut lawn and towered over her. She sipped iced tea, her fingers trembling as she set the glass down.

"I knew you'd come," she said. "Will you do it here?"

In all the turmoil of the last hour, Bess's words shook me. She thought I was going to kill her. She wiped a tear from her cheek and stared up at me.

"Is that what they told you I am? A monster? Diseased? You think that's what they said about Brady Langley? Did you know him?"

Bess let out a strangled cry. "I'm not responsible for that."

The moment she said it, I knew it was a lie. God. It was my fault. Bess Kennedy had been reporting on us all along. I sealed Molly's fate the minute I stepped out of the shadows behind the clinic. The weight of her betrayal threatened to crush me. But, as long as Molly and Keara still drew breath, there was time. Precious little.

"Zeke?" I asked. "You gonna tell me he made you do it?"

Bess closed her eyes against my words as if they would shield her from the pain of truth.

"How long has he been one of the Pack's spies?"

Bess's eyes snapped open. "I don't know. What difference does it make? Do you know who he reports to?"

"What do you know?" I went to her. I'm not proud, but I gripped her by the shoulders and shook her. I didn't hurt her. My touch was gentle, but Bess had been through so much, instinct made her flinch.

"You know what the Pack is, don't you? You've know it your whole life."

"It's you who doesn't know what the Pack is," she said. "Do you know who Zeke reports to? He's got this town on lock, Liam. The only man more powerful is the Alpha himself."

God. The answers had been right in front of me. I should have known it the moment I looked in Zeke Redmond's eyes that first night. He spied for the Alpha's top general. He was dialed into the true power in Shadow Springs. Now, he'd probably brought Molly and Keara right to him.

She openly wept now. "I didn't have a choice. I'm sorry about your friend, but they were going to hurt Molly. You couldn't protect her, so I did."

"What are you talking about? The Pack's taken Molly. God, I can feel them around her right now. Do you have any idea what it's doing to me not to charge over there?"

Bess rose slowly to her feet. "You're wrong. Zeke said they were interested in her friend Keara. That was the deal. Keara for Molly. I had no choice. They were going to kill her. She's going to hate me forever, but at least she'll be alive to do it."

I tore a hand through my hair. There was still a part of me that could step back and look at her from a distance. Removed from the pain Molly's distress caused me. "You made a deal with the Pack? You trusted them? Bess, they were never going to honor that."

She put a hand to her mouth. "What are you telling me?"

"I'm telling you you haven't saved Molly from anything."

"Oh, God. I swear to you. They promised. That was my condition."

I gripped the railing of her porch so hard the wood splintered. Bess jumped and took a step back. I tried to steady my breathing. She was terrified.

"It's not too late," I forced myself to say, hoping to God it was true. "It's not too late if you help me now. I know where they are. But I need to know how many of them there are. I need to know how deep this goes."

"What are you going to do? What *can* you do? His name is Tenley. I've only met him once. Zeke says there's no one more powerful than him except the Alpha."

Tenley. The name simmered in my brain. Rage boiled through me.

My vision tunneled and I knew she could see my wolf eyes. There was no help for it anymore. But, I could see her nature as easily as she could see mine. She was just a scared woman trying to do what she thought was right, misguided as that might be. She was also my only chance.

"There were three of them," she said. "This Tenley was with them. I've been around shifters before, Liam. But this one...he's different. Zeke brought them here in his truck. They made me tell them where Keara was going to meet Molly. I'm sorry, Liam. I set a meeting up between the two of them at the clinic. I have no idea if any more met them. I don't know where they've taken them."

I reached for her. Somehow, it seemed important to me to comfort her. It was as if I needed to remind myself that through all of that, I was still human too.

"It's all right," I said, though I knew it wasn't. "I do."

TWENTY-ONE

MOLLY

The light blinded me as the black hood was taken from my head. Strong hands shoved me down, forcing me to sit on a cheap folding chair. There was no need for bindings; I would never be able to move fast enough to outrun these men.

My head pounded. Instinct made me reach out, searching for Liam's steady heartbeat beating close to mine. But, the instant I did it, I regretted it. My captors took notice.

As my eyes adjusted to the light, I didn't even have to look to know who it was. Tenley, the fireman from the other night, towered over me. His wolf eyes glimmered from gold to red, then finally settled to a more human brown. My eyes went up and up. The power of his wolf radiated from him. He leaned against a pallet of cut wood, his black t-shirt stretched taut over ripped muscles. He had dark hair, black as night.

Shuffling to the left drew my attention. A door opened and another hooded figure stumbled into the room.

"Keara!" I should have stayed quiet. Why give these men any more than I had to? But Keara was hurt. As Tenley's companion tore off Keara's hood, blood poured from a deep gash over her left eye. She landed on all fours, her shoulders quaking. Oh, God. She'd been hit hard enough she was dizzy and disoriented.

Her own gaze traveled up as Tenley walked toward her. The heels of his cowboy boots hit the ground hard as he stopped in front of her. Naked lust came into his expression as he squatted down and hooked a hand beneath Keara's chin.

"Baby," he said. "I told you this wasn't going to work out for you the way you hoped."

Keara reared back and spit right in his face. Tenley didn't even flinch. When the two other men advanced, he held up a hand to stop them. I imagined he could give them orders on some tele-pathic level, but his body language read loud and clear. Whatever Keara's fate, he would deliver it.

Baby. He'd called her baby. A puzzle piece slammed into my brain with sickening clarity. Liam had said Keara had been promised to one of the Alpha's top generals. That general was currently staring straight at her, wiping her spittle from his cheek with the handkerchief he'd pulled from his back pocket.

When Tenley reached for her, I couldn't stay quiet. "Stop it! Take your hands off of her."

It was Keara who reacted. Her eyes locked with mine and her nostrils flared. God, she was so strong, so brave. She'd kept it all a secret. Tenley had been in Shadow Springs this whole time and yet she'd hidden the fact of who he was from Jagger. I knew why. She said he'd rip him apart.

Slowly, she drew herself to her feet. My heart broke as she stag-gered sideways, struggling to stay upright. It was Tenley who reached out to steady her. His touch was light, but Keara's whole body recoiled. She hissed in pain as if he'd burned her with acid.

Tenley's wolf eyes flashed. His touch became more forceful as he turned Keara. He smoothed his hand over her neck, pulling her hair up at the collar. Jagger's mark blazed bright. It looked nothing like what I saw the other day. Then, it had been healed over, barely more than a faint, white scar. Now, the flesh looked tender and pink, almost as if she were having some kind of allergic reaction to Tenley's touch. I realized I wasn't probably far off. Jagger was her Alpha. The touch of another wolf was anathema to her. Oh, God. In that fleeting instant, I wished I bore Liam's mark. As much as it caused Keara pain to have Tenley touch her, Keara's touch seemed abhorrent to him as well. He pushed her away from him.

"I'd say it's working out just fine for me," Keara said. She stayed on her feet. Her eyes darted to me and she straightened her back. If she could be brave, so could I.

"That's an Alpha's mark," Tenley said. "You're smart. You haven't told him about me, have you? He doesn't know what I am to you."

"You're nothing to me," Keara said, her tone flat.

He seemed to be having trouble staying on his own feet. Rage boiled through him, and a threatening growl vibrated through him. One of his companions reacted. His wolf burst forth. He advanced on Keara, teeth bared.

Tenley knocked him sideways with the back of his hand. The black wolf yelped and dropped his head. Tenley may not be *the* Alpha, but he was clearly in command of these two. The other man was the smallest of the three. He stayed human, but sweat poured from his brow. He came to me, jerking me to my feet. He brought me to Tenley.

My breath hitched. My thunderous heartbeat made me dizzy. I locked eyes with Keara. We drew strength from each other. I felt

Tenley's hot breath against my cheek. He licked his lips and slid his fingers to the back of my neck.

God. Oh, God.

The instant Tenley's flesh touched mine, a new pulse blazed to life between my ears. His. My knees buckled as I tried to drive it out. Tenley pulled my hair back, examining the base of my neck. He ran his thumb against the unmarred flesh he found there.

"She's clean," he said. He let me go but pressed the pad of his thumb to his front teeth.

He turned to Keara. "You think you're clever, Keara."

"Clever enough," she said. "It doesn't matter what happens to me, and you know it. I'll never be yours, and that's all that matters."

He laughed at her. "You're right. You think you dodged a bullet. Maybe you have. You think the Alpha can't find a way to remove that mark you bear? You think his *own* mark isn't stronger? Sure, you're second-hand goods now, but that might not matter to someone lesser than me."

"I told you I'd never mate with you," Keara said. "I remember making you that promise. You doubted me once. Maybe now you'll know not to do it again."

Tenley shrugged. "Looks like I don't need you for a mate anymore, Keara." He slid his hands to the back of my neck once more. "It looks like you've brought me another option."

Tenley got two equally violent reactions from his companions. The black wolf charged forward, teeth bared. Again, Tenley batted him away. The second man stepped forward; his wolf eyes flashed red.

"You don't get to decide that, Davis," he said. So Tenley had a first name. I filed it away. I might have been grateful for the seeming defense to my honor, but both the black wolf and the second man looked at me with predatory fury.

Tenley grabbed the man by the throat. His movements were so swift, so deadly, the air left my lungs right along with his victim's. He held him there against the wall. It was a direct challenge. The second man might clearly have been able to throw Tenley off. He had the same shifter strength cording his muscles. But, he stayed still, his feet dangling an inch off the ground.

"And you'll wait your turn like you were ordered, Mason."

Mason curled his fingers around Tenley's. Whatever psychic words they spoke to each other, it was enough to get Tenley to loosen his grip. Mason fell to the ground in a heap. He growled, but didn't challenge Tenley a second time.

Some detached, clinical part of my brain studied them. The structure of the Chief Pack was complex. Tenley was an Alpha, just like Jagger, Liam, Mac, Payne, and Gunnar. And yet, he was held in whatever thrall the Chief Alpha exerted. If I closed my eyes, I could almost feel it myself. There was a thickness surrounding them, almost as if they were joined with invisible chains. There was a pull. I'd felt it before with Liam. Any time the soldiers of the Chief Pack drew close, it weighed him down and threatened to drive away his reason.

So much power. So much malice. Tenley turned back to me.

"Molly," Keara's voice broke. "Don't let him. Don't touch her!"

Tenley's smile widened. He shot Keara a glance and came to me. I rose from the chair, facing him squarely. My heart thundered. My knees went weak. Oh, God. This man had a pull of his own. It was more restrained than Liam's. Liam's was wild, raw, exhilarating. Tenley's was more methodical and rhythmic...almost practiced. And yet, I was still drawn to it. I pushed the chair between us and took two steps back.

"Relax," Tenley said. I think he was talking both to Keara and Mason. "I'm not a rule breaker." He fixed his gaze on me, letting his wolf eyes rage to the surface.

"It'll be a relief to you," he said. "You'll see. You deserve a disciplined mate. You deserve to live in the light. I could make you my queen."

"You mark her now, the Alpha will kill you where you stand," Keara cried.

Tenley snapped his jaw and snarled. Perhaps he wasn't as disciplined as he wanted me to believe. His eyes went briefly red and I realized what I was seeing. Keara was right. The Alpha hold on him was strong.

I took in my surroundings for the first time. This was a large garage or warehouse. I could smell fresh cut lumber. Moonlight spilled in from two high windows. The steel door behind Tenley was shut tight.

"I should kill you where you stand, Keara," he said. "He wouldn't stop me from doing that."

"No," I shouted. We needed time. Keara's distress came not just from her physical injuries. Sweat poured between her breasts, darkening the front of her shirt. Liam said their bond was so much deeper than anything I could describe. Jagger could feel her pain and she could feel his. He must be in agony now. The others had to be restraining him somehow. It was the only thing that made sense. Because he would come for her. He would risk his own life and the lives of everyone in the caves to get to her.

A new chill snaked down my spine. Liam would do the same. But if he tried...if he got this close to these men...the Chief Pack would find him.

It seemed Keara and I had our own nonverbal link. I searched her face as a single tear fell down her cheek. The thing she and Jagger feared all along had finally come true. The Pack would use her against him.

"Davis," Mason said. "We have our orders. Let's quit dicking around. The Alpha wants us to flush out the traitor. Let's get it done."

Tenley hissed. He turned on Mason yet again. This time, the other man took a bold step toward him.

"Mason," Tenley said, softening his voice. "You think I'm crazy? I know what our orders are. Harris, you go outside and patrol. The minute you sense someone coming, you know what to do."

Harris, the black wolf, let out a keening whine, then dashed off into the shadows to patrol. In his wolf, he'd be the first to sense anyone approaching. With each passing moment, realization dawned that this could have no good outcome. Liam and the others couldn't overpower these shifters without tipping off the Pack. I didn't know exactly where we were, but I sensed we were too far for them to race to the safety of the caves. It meant Keara and I would have to find a way to either break free ourselves or buy more time.

Tenley came to me. "It's too late for her," he gestured toward Keara with his chin. "Well, I mean it's too late for her to find a decent mate after all this. That doesn't mean there won't be lesser wolves willing to settle for sloppy seconds. Granted, it won't be a pretty life for her. You, on the other hand. You're still unspoiled. Plus, you've been to their hideout, haven't you? I can smell those wolves on you."

He wrinkled his nose in disgust. My blood turned cold.

"That makes you a prize. The Alpha rewards those loyal to him. As soon as you're properly motivated, the things you know will be an asset. It's your lucky day, baby. What did she call you? Molly? Molly. I like it."

Tenley reached for me. I stayed stock still as he ran his finger along my jaw.

"I think you'll take to Birch Haven."

Birch Haven. It was just a word. A name. One I'd never heard before. But the moment he said it, tingling pain shot through me. Keara's eyes widened. The name meant something to her too.

"Come on, Davis," Mason said. "He wants us back."

Mason started to press the heel of his palm against his temple. Whatever mental powers the Pack exerted on him were starting to cause him physical pain. Tenley looked over his shoulder but stayed calm and still. Oh, he was an Alpha at his core. There could be no doubt. It gave me an idea.

"Doesn't it bother you taking orders from him all the time?" I said. Time. We needed time. I tried to even my breathing and keep my heartrate steady. Liam and I might not share a mate bond like Jagger and Keara did, but I knew he could find me in an instant if he needed to. So why hadn't he? There could be no other explanation than the stranglehold the Alpha had on these men. If Liam and the others walked into it, we were lost.

I shot a pointed glance to Keara. I didn't like the looks of the gash on her forehead. It still bled freely and the edges of it were jagged. She took a halting step sideways, coming to rest against the pallet of wood in the center of the room. Mason moved toward her. His nose twitched as the scent of her blood worked on him.

"She's not so bad, Davis," he said.

"Not for someone like you," Tenley answered. "You want me to put a good word in for you with Mr. Valent?"

"Don't!" Mason clapped his hands over his ears. "Don't call him that. He hates it when you call him that."

Tenley laughed. He was toying with Mason.

"Valent," I said. "Is that his name? Your Alpha?"

Mason growled. His nose twitched and his skin bristled. He was having a tough time staying human. I couldn't decide whether that worked for or against us. Valent. The name had power, just like Birch Haven did.

"We got to *go*, Davis!"

"We go when I say we go."

Keara rallied. "Who are you trying to impress, Tenley?" she asked. "Molly's never going to let you claim her unless you do it by force."

He raised a brow and turned to her. "Well, that's kind of the fun of it, Keara. So, how is he anyway? Huh? Jagger Wilkes? That's who you spread it for?"

Keara's face went white. Tenley's spread in a wicked smile. "Ah. That's what I figured. He's got a cousin with him, too."

"Come *on*, Davis!" Mason had turned. He was mumbling something to himself and walking in circles near Keara. The Alpha had to be screaming inside his head. Why wasn't it impacting Tenley in the same way? He was stronger, clearly.

I made a gamble. I went to Tenley and raised my hand. I pressed it to his cheek. He caught it and held it there. His skin flared hot beneath my fingers. My pulse raced, but with danger, not desire. To Tenley, I wasn't sure he understood the difference.

"What kind of life is this for you?" I whispered. Maybe Mason would have been able to hear me under normal circumstances. As it was, the voice in his head seemed to drown everything else out.

Tenley grew bold and pressed his lips to my palm. I steadied my breathing, fighting back the urge to pull away. I'd judged correctly. Lust coursed through him, glinting in his eyes.

"You're an Alpha, that's why my touch burns through you. I'm an

Alpha's mate. You've got that part figured out. But, I'm not *your* mate. She's out there somewhere though. Isn't she? Isn't that how it works? You each have a fated mate. You could find her. We could help you. You could choose for yourself."

Tenley's lips curled. He started to salivate. Oh, I'd reached him all right.

"You're an *Alpha*," I whispered, bringing my lips within an inch of his ear. "Why are you willing to settle? You don't have to. We can show you the way."

Over Tenley's shoulder, Keara grew very still. She'd once told me I was a natural born recruiter. She'd meant Bess. My pulse quickened. Bess had betrayed us. Why else had these men shown up in Zeke's truck? He was nowhere to be found. I wondered if he stood guard outside with the black wolf, Harris. What had they promised him to get him to cooperate? What had they promised Bess?

I couldn't think about that now. The sting of Bess's treachery burned deep. Now, I had to gather my wits and play out the game I'd started.

"Is there someplace we can talk in private?" I asked, my eyes darting to Mason. He paced in front of Keara. Her eyes widened with renewed alarm as she watched me with Tenley. More than anything, I wished I could communicate with her the way the shifters did.

Tenley took the bait. He tightened his fingers around my wrist and pulled me into a darkened corner of the warehouse. I couldn't help screaming out. Keara called for me. I recovered and straightened my back.

Tenley had my back up against the wall. His teeth grazed my cheek and he licked me. "You taste wild," he said. "But not fully spoiled yet."

"But, you know I'm not yours no matter how much you want me to be. Davis, your mate *is* out there somewhere. I can help you find her. Isn't that better than taking...what was it...sloppy seconds that Mr. Valent orders you to? You weren't born for this. Why deny your true nature? This is the old way. Let me help you find a better one. It's right. It's natural, and you know it. Do you really want a second-rate mate that's not intended for you? To what end? You saw what Brady was. Do you want a son like him?"

It was pitch black in this corner of the warehouse except for Tenley's glowing eyes. As long as they stayed gold, I knew I had a foothold. Desire made him tremble. It called to my nature at the same time I recoiled from it. I *was* an Alpha's mate, after all. I realized with growing alarm that *my* Alpha was nearby.

Liam.

Oh, God. Liam. I prayed he had the strength to fight off the Chief Alpha's pull. The conduit of that pull stood an inch away from me. He realized what I did at the same instant. Baring his teeth, he licked me once again.

"Tick tock," Tenley said. "Time's up. I knew they couldn't stay away. What makes you so special, little Molly? And think of how much fun we're going to have finding out together."

"Davis!" Mason's voice grew desperate.

"In a minute!" Tenley hollered.

But hell had already broken loose. Liam's pulse thundered in my ears. My flesh seared where Tenley gripped me. He felt the change in my body heat and his lips curled back in a smile. He jerked me forward, dragging me back to the main part of the warehouse.

I could hear the black wolf yelp with pain then grow deadly silent. The wolves were all around.

But none of it mattered. Not a single thing. Mason stood in the center of the room. He had Keara by the throat.

"Mason, don't!" For the first time since he brought us here, Tenley sounded scared. Mason was caught between his wolf and his man. He closed his hands around Keara's neck. Her eyes locked with mine.

"No!" I shouted. Tenley screamed it too.

But, Mason was too far gone. His teeth bared, he jerked his hands around Keara's neck, snapping it. No longer able to hold off his wolf, he shifted. The force of Mason's shift flung Keara cruelly against the wall.

TWENTY-TWO

LIAM

Jagger might never forgive us. I knew in my heart he would blame me most of all. My cousin. My blood. We bound him in chains made of dragonsteel and left to try and save his heart.

My own heart ripped from me as we got closer to the warehouse. Molly was strong. I could feel her trying to keep calm. Even now, she was trying to protect me.

"You okay, man?" Payne asked. We'd belly-crawled up a shallow embankment. The warehouse was bordered by a small reservoir. Bess's intel had been accurate so far. We sensed three shifters from the Pack. One strong, two weaker.

Gritting my teeth, I nodded at Payne. "We clear on what we're here to do?"

This was a kill mission. Once we got the girls to safety, we could leave no survivors, even if we were the ones to die.

"Why haven't they scented us yet?" Mac slid closer to me. His wolf eyes flashed in the dark stillness of the night.

I closed my eyes and reached out with my heart. Molly was moving, talking. Afraid, but in control.

"They aren't trying to yet," I said. Mac took it as the simple answer it sounded like. Payne shot me a look. He understood. They weren't trying because their attention was diverted by something.

Our women.

"Liam," Gunnar put a firm hand on my shoulder. It had nearly come to blows between us back in the caves. He'd lobbied to put me in chains right alongside Jagger. He figured my connection to Molly was strong enough to cloud my judgment and risk exposing all of us. I'd convinced him otherwise. I had lied.

"What do you see?" I said, my words thick in my throat.

Gunnar set his gaze toward the warehouse. Zeke's pickup truck was parked in front of it. Two red eyes flashed near the southwest corner. He was a big, black wolf. My skin pricked, but the wolf turned away from us.

"You see that fucker in the front seat?" Mac asked.

Squinting, I looked again at the truck. Sure enough, Zeke Redmond sat with his hands on the wheel looking nervously toward the prowling black wolf.

"We take the black wolf out first," Gunnar said.

"We split up," I countered. "The minute we make a move toward him, he'll alert the other two inside."

"Fine," Mac said. "You handle the black wolf and that shitheel in the pickup. Gunnar, Payne, and I will storm the warehouse."

I rose and faced him. "I'm going for Molly."

"Dammit, Liam," Gunnar tore a hand through his hair. "You let us handle it."

"I'm going for Molly," I said. "If I have to go through the three of you to get to her. I won't make a mistake."

"There's no time for this," Payne said. "But let this be a lesson to all of us. Mates are trouble."

"He's on her!" I shouted. I didn't wait for the others. I ran toward the northeast corner of the building. Gunnar and Payne swore behind me, but they followed.

Mac moved, but stayed behind, watching our sixes. All it would take was one wrong move and these wolves could signal to the rest of the Chief Pack. If more came, none of us would make it out alive.

Payne took the black wolf. He wasn't ready for it. Payne leaped and shifted in midair. He had the black wolf on his back, paws up. I tasted blood in my own mouth as Payne's fangs sank into his neck. I would have liked to watch him die.

An echoing click drew my attention. Zeke had gotten out of his truck. He aimed a shotgun straight at me. Gunnar was at my side, growling. He hadn't shifted yet, but his shoulders twitched with the urge.

"Like clockwork," Zeke said. Payne's attack had been almost silent. Earbuds dangled from Zeke's neck. The idiot hadn't seen or heard Payne strike. He hadn't realized that his wolf protector just had his throat ripped out.

Payne stood right behind Zeke, his fangs still dripping from the blood of his kill.

"Put the gun down, Zeke," I said. "We don't kill humans unless we have to. Don't make us have to."

Zeke shifted his aim, leveling the barrel of his shotgun straight at my chest. Payne struck before he got the shot off. Again, his attack came lethal and silent. But Zeke didn't die. His back broken, he writhed on the ground.

I stepped over him. "You shouldn't hit girls, Zeke," I said, spitting on the ground next to him.

"They're going to kill you." His voice came out as a painful hiss. But there was nothing more he could do. If he survived the night, he might never walk again.

She screamed. My heart turned to stone.

I heard Mac cry out from behind me, warning me not to move. Beneath that, the pull began low in my belly. They were close. They were coming.

My wolf tore out of me. I leaped high, shifting before my paws hit the ground. Payne and Gunnar were at my side. Pushing past me, they hit the steel door of the warehouse together, buckling it as if it were made of tinfoil. Their wolves rippled below the surface, but they held back the shift. I was too far gone.

In my mind, there was only Molly. For the rest of my life I would wonder if things might have ended differently if that hadn't been true. If I had held back my shift, would that have made the events of those three seconds change?

He held her against the back wall of the warehouse, his fingers curled around her neck. Molly's eyes widened with shock, but somehow, she didn't scream.

He was tall and broad; his eyes glinted gold. Not red. It meant he was as strong as we were. The Alpha's pull hadn't dragged him under, turning his eyes red. In my periphery I saw the red wolf. He'd shifted the instant we burst through the door. Payne, Gunnar, and Mac were on him.

Behind me, flesh tore. In my rage, I had no thought of whose it was. It didn't matter. Molly was the only thing that mattered.

"Stop!" Molly's voice reached me.

The pulse of the pack thundered inside my head. The command was simple.

Submit. Submit. Submit.

The urge to lie on the ground made my legs weak. Madness threatened to rip my vision from me. It was Molly's voice, Molly's heartbeat that tethered me.

Let her go! It was *my* command. The man holding her by the throat stayed still as a statue. Growls erupted behind me. It might have been the others. It might have been the red wolf. I didn't care.

"Liam," Molly whispered. "Oh, Liam." Her eyes fixed on a point over my left shoulder.

Something was coming. Hell, the whole Pack might be about to barge through the warehouse door. It didn't matter. It only mattered that I ripped apart the shifter standing between Molly and me.

"Don't call them," she cried. She wasn't talking to me. She was talking to the man holding her. "I'll go with you. Just don't call them. Let him go."

He turned to her, his lips curled into a smile. "You'll go with me anyway."

I didn't let him say anything more. Molly screamed as she turned back to me. She felt my thundering heartbeat and knew what I was about to do.

I lunged for him. He didn't shift then. If he had, he might have won. We might have died together.

As I sunk my teeth into his arm and pulled him off Molly, he cried out and tried to throw me off. When we tumbled to the ground together, only then did he shift. His wolf sprang forth. He was silvery-gray and bigger than me. In another time, another place, that might have mattered. But I had something to fight for.

"Liam!" Molly screamed.

The gray wolf rounded on me. I'd wounded him badly. Blood poured freely from the torn flesh of his shoulder. He got his bearings though and charged. He caught me in the chest, driving me backward until we hit the far wall of the warehouse. Metal buckled from the force of our bodies. I dug my claws into his back. He howled in agony but sank his teeth into my shoulder, drawing blood that made my vision waver.

I held on, going for his jugular. He squirmed beneath me. His greater size didn't matter as I held him down. His eyes went wide with understanding just before I sank my fangs in for the kill.

"Liam!" It was Mac's voice behind me. He needn't have worried. I knew what he wanted. The gray wolf's eyes darkened then began to fill with red. He was calling for the Chief Pack. The taste of metal filled my mouth as his blood began to flow.

He died with his eyes open, glinting gold still, but vacant.

My blood rage thundered through my veins. It wasn't enough that he was dead. I wanted to tear him apart. Strong hands on my shoulders drew me back. In the heat of it, I kept fighting. I would have kept on killing.

Once again, it was Molly's voice that drew me back from the brink.

"Liam," she cried. "Stop! It's Payne!"

I paused long enough for Payne to fling me against the wall. It got me out of my head long enough. I shifted back, rising on unsteady legs. Pain flared from the wound in my shoulder. Each pulse was agony.

Staggering forward, I looked for Molly. Panic seized me as I couldn't find her at first. Only Payne's hand on my good shoulder kept me from shifting again.

"We have to get out of here," he said. "You killed the strong one. But the Pack senses something. Can't you feel it?"

I couldn't feel anything but the pain in my shoulder and Molly's frantic heartbeat. Mac and Gunnar were doubled over near the center of the room though. Mac clamped his hands over his ears. The command from the Pack was burning through him.

Then I saw Molly. I had one brief beat of joy. Then, I took a step forward and my heart ripped in two.

She was on her knees, doubled over like the others. Her breath was ragged and she knelt over Keara. Keara lay on her back, not moving as Molly did chest compressions.

Oh, God.

I ran to Molly's side. Keara's color was ashen. Her eyes were fixed and dilated as she stared at the ceiling, sightless.

TWENTY-THREE

MOLLY

J agger was not my Alpha. Liam had not yet marked me. I was only human. Still, as we neared the mouth of the caves, Jagger's soulcry filled my head and drove me to my knees.

It was Liam who carried Keara to him. When I tried to follow, Mac put a hand on my shoulder and stopped me.

"It's not safe," he whispered. "Jagger's not himself."

Jagger wasn't himself. That sentence echoed through me, hollowing me out. I saw a glimpse of him before Mac and the others pulled me back. Half-man. Half-wolf. He was stuck in some in-between place, his bones jutting at wrong angles, his skin sallow and slack. But, it was his eyes that seared me most of all. They were not the pure gold of his wolf, not the fiery red that glinted when the Chief Pack took hold. They were coal black, almost as if someone had reached in and ripped the orbs out. Anything to spare him the vision of Liam bringing his mate to him.

He would have killed Liam. That was plain. Heavy chains held him back. He strained so hard against them the veins bulged from his temples.

"Come on," Mac said. "Let's leave them be."

Each step to Liam's cavern sent pain shooting through my heart. We passed the main rotunda and Keara's refugees. They already knew her fate. They stood with silent tears staining their faces. I knew by instinct that they had known the moment she died. Jagger's grief had torn through the cave walls.

"You're all right?" Mac asked. I sank slowly into the pallet of blankets Liam slept on. His scent comforted me. I gathered the top blanket, wrapping it around my shoulders.

Mac's eyes were kind, though edged in sorrow like all of ours. "It was so fast," I whispered. "It happened so fast."

I wondered if the vision of Keara breaking against the wall would ever leave me. For now, it stayed branded behind my eyes. In the end, Tenley had tried to stop it. He knew Keara was more valuable to the Alpha alive than dead. But, Mason had gone fully feral. Keara had been too close to him. Oh, God.

"I'm so sorry," he said. "We never should have let the two of you make that drop alone."

"You had no choice. Oh, Mac, none of us ever had any choice. It was my fault. I trusted the wrong person." My last words came out in a sobbing hiccup.

As if my guilt conjured her forth, a shadow darkened the mouth of the cavern and Bess stood there. Tears stained her cheeks as well. Mac growled and turned on her.

I hated her. I blamed her. And yet, she was just as much a victim in all of this. It was my turn to put a steadying hand on Mac.

"I'm so sorry," she said. "This wasn't supposed to happen."

Mac shook his head and let out a bitter laugh. "It's what comes from trusting the Pack. You're lucky it wasn't you who died."

"I wish it had been," she sobbed, leaning against the cave wall. If she wanted sympathy from me, I wasn't ready to give it.

She did get it though. My heart thundered and broke as Liam came to her side. He put a hand on Bess's shoulder. "You'll blame yourself," he said. "I can't stop you. There's enough blame to go around for all of us."

Mac acted quickly, ushering Bess away leaving Liam and me alone. I pulled the blanket tighter around my shoulders. My vision wavered as my eyes filled with tears. At the same time, my heart soared.

Liam was my Alpha. He had not yet marked me. But his soul still filled mine.

He came to me, breaking. Sinking to his knees before me, I gathered my arms around him and pulled him to my breast.

"He'll die," he whispered. "I'm afraid Jagger will die."

I kissed the top of his head. I had no answers. Slow tears fell from my eyes as I held Liam close. I never wanted to let him go again. His shoulders wracked with violent sobs. They were for Keara. They were for me. Finally, he tilted his face toward mine. I smoothed my thumbs over his strong cheekbones. Then, I leaned down and kissed him.

My heart mixed with guilt and love. Liam came for me. I never doubted it. My heart soared to be near him. But, the loss of Keara was so great.

"She wouldn't want that," I whispered. "She wouldn't want any of this. Keara knew the risks. She believed they were worth it."

"Tenley," he said. "His name was Tenley."

I nodded. "Yes. One of the Alpha's top generals. He kept the Pack at bay. I don't know how or why."

Liam straightened. He sat beside me on the ledge. "He wanted something more." Liam's tone darkened. Those last few moments with Tenley replayed in my brain.

"He wanted me," I said. "I taunted him. Liam, I could see it in his eyes. He was fighting the pull of the Pack. He was tempted by the thought of freedom and choosing for himself. Oh, God, I *felt* it burning through him. Why didn't they come? Why aren't we all dead now? Why aren't you and the others back under Pack control?"

Liam ran a hand over his face. "The Alpha can't control the entire Pack alone. He uses his top men to control territories for him. It must have been up to Tenley to make the call to the rest of the Pack. You stopped him from doing it, Molly. My brave, strong, Molly. Oh, God, do you know how close I came to losing you? I'm selfish for feeling it, but God help me, I'm relieved."

He sobbed against my shoulder. "I'm relieved it wasn't you."

"Shh." I kissed him and pulled him close. "I know. I know."

"If anything had happened to you. It would kill me, baby. I love you. You've seen what it's doing to Jagger. I can't let that happen to you. I won't let…"

I straightened my back and held Liam's gaze. I knew what he was going to say. I also knew what I needed to say.

"Liam," I said. "When Tenley…touched me…he could have marked me. He wanted to. If he had, you and I both know what would have happened. He would have been able to make me betray you. And Keara…did you know Davis Tenley was the general she was meant for?"

Liam reared back. "She told you?"

"They both told me."

Liam put his face in his hands. "Then why didn't he just take her? At least she'd be alive. At least we'd have a chance to try and get her back."

"Jagger's mark repelled him. That's what I'm trying to tell you. Liam, and I...we belong together. I never want to be put at risk like that again."

"I know," he said. "Baby, I know. I'll figure out a way. I'm sorry. I'll make a plan to send you far away. Michigan, maybe. Over into Canada would be even better…"

"Liam, no. That's not what I'm saying. I'm saying I don't want to do this halfway anymore. In spite of all of it, I know where I belong. And that's with you. Forever. Baby, I love you. I want you to mark me. Claim me."

Liam pulled away. He bolted to his feet. As the man inside of him tried to search for logic, the beast within him flared with desire. His eyes flashed gold.

"Molly."

"I've made up my mind. It's what Keara would want, and you know it."

"No. You can be safe now, Molly. You can walk away from all of it. Tenley and his companions are dead. The Pack doesn't know about you."

I stood, facing him. "But, I know about the Pack. Liam, we've only just begun. If I leave now, everything Keara fought and died for will be in vain. There are others like her and like me. Women marked and taken against their will. Tenley mentioned a place...Birch Haven. I think it's where they send them. It meant something to Keara."

Liam didn't get a chance to answer me. Payne and Gunnar came to the cavern opening. Grief still colored their expressions, but there was something else there too.

"Liam," Payne said. "I think you need to come with us. Just for a few minutes."

He looked back at me. Payne and Gunnar hadn't invited me along, but I decided at that moment that I wasn't leaving Liam's side. I clasped my hand in his and squared my shoulders. Payne and Gunnar exchanged a look, but they made no move to stop me. I'd fought just as hard as they had today.

We walked out of the cavern together. Payne led the way up the passageways until we emerged into the deepest part of Mammoth Forest.

The sky had gone from inky black to pink. Dawn had come.

Mac was already topside. He stood with his hand gripping a tall poplar a few yards away. When he turned, his eyes flashed silver.

"Listen," he said. "Do you hear it?"

Liam bristled beside me. His heartbeat tripped right along with mine. Slowly, he inhaled and let his eyes go hooded. One beat. Two. Peace settled over him. I squeezed his hand.

"What is it?" I whispered.

"The link," he said, snapping his eyes open. "It's broken."

"Not broken," Mac said, coming toward us. "But it's definitely grown weaker. The Pack's moved off or something."

"No," Payne said. "They're not gone. Not all the way."

"No," Liam's voice dropped. "But we sure as shit made a dent."

"Is it because of Tenley?"

"I think so," Liam answered.

So, we had a greater war to fight. But today, a battle had been won.

Payne and Gunnar moved away from us. They dropped to all fours and shifted. I'd never seen their wolves in daylight. Payne's was russet with flecks of gold through his fur. His green eyes shone like emeralds. Beside him, Gunnar's wolf was pale silver, almost platinum.

They howled and ran up an embankment on the other side of the small stream flowing near our feet. When they reached the top of the hill, Payne and Gunnar threw their heads back, howling in unison.

It was a mourning cry. My skin pricked and my blood heated. Liam stirred beside me. I gave him a nod and he dropped my hand. He shifted then joined the others. Mac was soon to follow.

Four wolves stood shoulder to shoulder, their majestic silhouettes cut into the horizon. Their howls honored one fallen warrior and the one she'd left behind. I felt Liam's vow vibrating through him, a promise to Jagger. To me. Keara would not die in vain. She would be avenged. She would be set free.

TWENTY-FOUR

Liam

I let her walk ahead of me, enjoying the set of her shoulders and her strong back as she found the place. I hadn't told her where to go. Instinct drew her.

We waited until the moon was full again. It seemed fitting to let a month pass. Now, it could be more *our* time, not a decision made in the haste of grief. If I ever thought Molly viewed it as such, she proved me wrong tonight. When she reached the clearing near the deepest part of the stream, she turned to face me.

Her pale skin shimmered beneath the moonlight. A breeze kicked up. She should be cold here. The leaves had already begun to turn and we'd had the first snowfall last week. Molly held her hand out to mine; her smile lit me from the inside out.

"You're sure." I'd said it a thousand times. There was never any need. I could sense it in the way she breathed, the way she squared her shoulders, and the strong, steady beat of her heart.

My heart. My love.

She went up on her tiptoes. I tilted my head down and kissed her. I could be gentle now. In another moment, I wouldn't be. Even now, the strength of the pull between us stirred my wolf. My vision darkened and I knew she could see the golden glint of the beast she'd grown to love.

"I love you," she whispered. Molly tasted like sweet cinnamon. Her heart throbbed. I trailed my fingers down her arm, loving the gooseflesh I made. I took a step back, wanting to admire her again.

Her nipples peaked. I reached for one of them, tweaking it. She threw her head back and groaned. I didn't have to tell her what to do.

Molly sank to the soft earth. Her full lips parted in a wicked smile. She let her thighs fall to the side. Her sex glistened with the dew of desire. I could watch her like that forever. Without even thinking, Molly reached between her legs, drawing a finger between her slick folds. Her breath hitched as she stroked herself for me.

"Baby," I whispered, dropping to my knees before her. It seemed fitting that I did. I wanted to worship at her feet. Molly's scent reached me. More cinnamon mixed with darker lust, mingling with the woodland smells that drew me home.

I pressed my palms against her thighs, spreading her wide. I licked my lips, loving the way she squirmed in anticipation. I couldn't help myself. I wanted to tease her, draw her out. She'd begged me time and again for this, but I couldn't get enough of it. She tasted so good.

"Liam!" She gasped, threading her fingers through my hair as I drew her out. She bucked and writhed beneath me. I nipped her thigh. She went still except for the hitch of her breath. I loved the way it made her breasts quiver.

"Liam," she said. "Please. I can't wait."

"Oh, yes, you can. You can do anything I ask of you."

She threw her head back and moaned. I was a liar, anyway. I was just as eager as she was. She thrust her hips forward, beckoning me to use my tongue on her again. I did. I flicked that sweet little bud until it grew hard beneath my touch. Then, I knew she'd reached her breaking point.

"Not yet," I said, nipping her thigh again. She squirmed, but went still. I slid my hand beneath her buttocks, gently urging her to turn.

She did. Her legs shuddering, she went on all fours. Molly dropped her head, letting her hair fall to the side. My dick was rock hard for her. Every part of my nature demanded this. I felt my fangs come out. Leaning forward, I grazed her shoulder with them. Molly gasped with pleasure. I slid my hand between her legs. She was wet. Dripping.

I stroked myself, edging my cock between her legs. Molly dug her fingers into the soft earth to brace herself.

"Hold still," I cautioned her again.

She gasped, kicking up a grouse from the nearby brush. Its wings fluttered. So did Molly. I worked my fingers between her legs, stroking her, coaxing her to the edge once again.

"Liam! I can't hold back!"

My wicked laughter brushed her temple. "Yes, you can, baby."

But, it was me who couldn't hold back. I took two fingers and spread her wide, easing my passage. Molly cried out as I entered her. This was different and she felt it instantly.

"Oh! Oh! Baby! You're bigger. How are you bigger?"

"Shh," I cautioned. I sheathed myself to the root. Molly arched her back to receive me. I filled her wholly, completely as she stretched even wider to accommodate me. She was right. This was different than every other time. Because this time, I would make her mine.

I started the slow, ancient rhythm. Instinctively, Molly responded. She dropped her chin to the ground, angling her ass up even higher, taking me deeper. I thrust inside her again and again.

Her moans of pleasure echoed through the forest. Oh, God. I knew how lucky we were to have these stolen moments. Just a few weeks ago, this ritual would have drawn the Pack. It would again, I knew. But not tonight.

I felt Molly stretch and quiver against me. My own powerful build threatened to unseat me. It was almost time. Molly picked up the rhythm, thrusting back; she fucked me wild and raw. Her grunts grew louder.

"That's it, baby," I said. "Take it. Scream if you have to. We own the night."

And we did.

Molly threw her head back. Her hair dropped to the side again, exposing the nape of her neck. I swelled within her. She shrieked with delight. Then, I couldn't hold back a second longer. Stretching myself long, I reached for her. I held her still with one hand on her shoulder. Then, I sank my teeth into the sweet spot at the base of her neck. Marking her. Tasting her.

"Yes!" Molly cried. "Oh my God! Yes!"

I knew what she felt because I felt it too. As I made my Alpha's Mark, Molly felt pleasure there just like the throbbing pulse between her legs. It was as if she now had two erogenous zones, forever connected. She would burn for me there. In time, I would mark her again and again. Each coupling would bind her closer to me. There would come a time when we wouldn't need words to communicate no matter how far apart we were.

She was mine. I was hers. I claimed her that night. Totally. Completely. Forever.

Molly's pleasure exploded around me. I couldn't stop. I bit her once again, sealing the mark and wiping the blood away. By the time I took her in my arms, it would already be healed. As she shuddered out the last spasms of pleasure, mine began.

"Yes!" Molly cried out again, craving my seed. On a night like this, I could even dare to hope that someday, we could let it take root. We could bring a new generation of shifters into the world who would live free as they were supposed to. That night, it seemed everything was possible.

And it was all because of this marvel of a woman beneath me. As I spent myself inside her, Molly sank into me, sighing out my name.

Then, I did hold her close. I took her in my arms and left a trail of soft kisses around her breasts, in the hollow of her throat, until I finally found her lips.

"I love you," she said. "My God. Why did we wait so long?"

Laughing, I brushed the hair from her face. Molly's heart beat with my heart. The bond was sealed and it was strong. I felt a twinge of fear at that. For the first time, I could fully appreciate what Jagger was now. If anything happened to rip this bond from me, I wouldn't want to go on.

Molly's face darkened. She knew what I was thinking and she shared my fear. But, my brave girl reached up and touched my face.

"We'll survive," she whispered. "We've come this far. It's a new beginning, Liam. Whatever happens next, this was worth it. Just this moment."

Smiling, I drew her close. "Of course it is. I love you, baby." I brought her palm to my lips and kissed it.

My Molly. My love. My heart.

She was right. While my heart beat alongside hers, everything was possible.

EPILOGUE

Molly

Six months later...

As always, I felt Liam before I heard him. I stood in the center of the cavern rotunda. A new shipment of food and medical supplies had arrived. Dr. Bess had taken charge of them, barking orders like a regular drill sergeant as her new interns scurried around at her command. She shot me a conspiratorial wink when they weren't looking.

Liam's strong arms came around me. I leaned back, resting my head against his chest in the spot where I fit best.

"Things still quiet topside?" I asked.

He nodded and kissed my cheek. "For now. We think there will be a new general installed somewhere near Shadow Springs by the end of the summer."

My heart dropped. It was news I'd been expecting. We knew we'd been on borrowed time through Christmas. But, Tenley's demise had given us the window of time we needed to strengthen and rebuild the network Keara started.

"I still can't believe how much you've done in such a short amount of time," Liam said.

Funny, I barely stopped to think of it myself. It never seemed like there was time. Bess and I had gone back to work at the clinic. Business as usual except I'd started classes toward my D.V.M. I knew the time would come when we'd need more than one doctor around here. We were working on finding M.D. surgeons to join our ranks too. Bess had some leads.

"Come on," I said. "Let me show you the new setup."

I took Liam by the hand. He and the others had finished clearing out more passageways and caverns to the east. We had two more miles of space. We'd made barracks, a sort of mess hall, and an infirmary. Bess had been in charge of the last bit. She'd outfitted it with examination tables, enough medical supplies to last two years, and her masterpiece, a fully functioning operating room.

"Looks amazing," Liam said. "I wish I could say we'll never need it."

I reached up and touched his cheek, smoothing away the lines of worry. "And maybe we won't."

"How're Jason and Michael doing with the new borders?" Liam asked.

Three months ago, I'd taken a chance and brought the pair of them down to the caves. Michael had been a godsend. He used his National Guard staff sergeant training to bring order from chaos. We currently had thirty refugees down in the caves. Most of them were on their way across the border. A few of them would stay. With each new escape, we put a crack in the hold the Chief Pack had. I liked to think that each one would bring us closer to liberation day for all of the Kentucky shifters.

"Any change today?" I asked. I'd been asking the same thing for weeks now.

Liam shrugged. "He's taking food again at least."

I set down the clipboard I'd been holding against my chest. "What does Mac say?"

Liam's face grew dark. This had been a sore spot for us. Before he could answer, Mac himself rounded the corner and emerged from the passageway in front of us. He stopped short, seeing Liam and me. He knew exactly what I would ask him.

"Are you sure about this?" I said, going to Mac's side.

He gave me a sheepish grin and a quick hug. "We've been over this. I'm better off alone."

Mac finally found what he thought was a break in the mystery of Birch Haven. He refused to tell me any more. There was an unspoken rule that Liam and I would stay away from some of the more sensitive details of some of the group's missions. It was safer for all of them if we had compartmental knowledge in the event either of us ended up in enemy hands. I shuddered and pushed the thought out of my mind.

Mac had a chance to do real good. He hoped to find Birch Haven and liberate the women who had been taken there. I knew he was hoping he'd find his sister, Lena too. I said the same silent prayer for his success and safety.

Mac was leaving. I'd stocked him with supplies myself. I wanted him to wait just a few more days. I had a lead on a new vehicle for him. But, we both knew I was only stalling.

Knowing my mind as he always did, Liam rubbed my shoulder. "It's now or never, Moll. Mac needs to be long gone before there's a new general in Shadow Springs."

My eyes filled with tears at the thought of not seeing him again. There were never any guarantees. Keara had taught us all that.

"I know. I was just hoping Jagger would be well enough to go with you. A look passed between them. I knew what they were thinking. There was a chance Jagger might never be well again. He ate. He slept. Beyond that, he was catatonic. We'd taken him up to the forest, hoping the air might bring out his wolf, but it hadn't worked.

"Time," Mac said. "He just needs more time." His tone held authority we all knew he didn't have. We were all just guessing and hoping for the best where Jagger was concerned.

"Just be careful," I told Mac for the thousandth time. Since Liam marked me, I'd grown so close to all my Mammoth Forest wolves. They were like the brothers I'd never had. I knew why Keara was willing to die for them. Because, I would too.

Mac hugged me and smoothed my hair back. "I'll see you soon," he said. It's what we all said to each other when we parted. Never goodbye. It seemed like bad luck.

Liam and I walked to the edge of the passageway with him. I drew strength from him as I waved goodbye to Mac one last time. We watched as he disappeared into the light of day. I swallowed back my sense of foreboding.

"Shh," Liam said, shaking me gently. "Mac can take care of himself. We have to have hope. Think positive."

Smiling up at him, I went up on my tiptoes and kissed him. "I am. I promise."

We heard a shout and a crash from deeper in the cavern. A string of obscenities flew from Jason's mouth. Liam and I laughed together.

"Come on, baby," he said. "Before he hurts himself."

Liam took my hand and led me back into the caves. Love filled my heart as I turned and walked by Liam's side. Whatever came, we would face it together. I stole one last glance over my shoulder, letting the sunlight fall on my face. He was right. It felt just like hope.

The End

UP NEXT FROM KIMBER WHITE...

Thank you so much for taking this ride with Liam and Molly. I've been waiting to get these stories out for years. I have so much more planned for this series. Up next, we'll follow Mac on his quest to find his missing sister. Infiltrating Birch Haven won't be an easy task. What he finds there will bring him face to face with the darkest secrets the Kentucky Chief Pack harbors. When he runs into the gorgeous Eve, her feisty spirit and stubborn fire stirs his inner wolf in every way he doesn't need. Plus, she's marked for another. Being near her will put Mac's heart and life on the line. Don't miss Mac, Mammoth Forest Wolves Book Two. You can get more information about Mac at http://www.kimberwhite.-com/mammoth-forest-wolves/mac.

For a first look at my next new release, sign up for my newsletter today. You'll be the first to know about my new releases and special discounts available only to subscribers. You'll also get a FREE EBOOK right now, as a special welcome gift for joining. I promise not to spam you, share your email or engage in other general assholery. You can unsubscribe anytime you like (I'll only cry a little). You can sign up here! http://www.kimberwhite.-com/newsletter-signup

Psst . . . can I ask you a favor?

If you liked this story, can you do something for me? Please consider leaving a review. Reviews help authors like me stay visible and allow me to keep bringing you more stories. Reviews are the fuel that keeps us going. Please and thank you.

And if you STILL want more, I'd love to hang out with you on Facebook. I like to share story ideas, casting pics, and general insanity on a regular basis.

From the bottom of my heart though, THANK YOU for your support. You rock hard.

See you on the wild side!

Kimber

KimberWhite.com

kimberwhiteauthor@gmail.com

BOOKS BY KIMBER WHITE

Mammoth Forest Wolves

Liam

Mac

Gunnar

Payne

Jagger

Wild Lake Wolves Series

Rogue Alpha

Dark Wolf

Primal Heat

Savage Moon

Hunter's Heart

Wild Lake Wolves Prequel Novels

Wild Hearts

Stolen Mate

Wild Ridge Bears Series

Lord of the Bears (featuring Jaxson)

Outlaw of the Bears (featuring Cullen)

35304948R00142

Made in the USA
Middletown, DE
04 February 2019